MYSTERY OF SMUGGLERS COVE

THE HARDY BOYS™ MYSTERY STORIES

MYSTERY OF SMUGGLERS COVE

Franklin W. Dixon

Illustrated by Leslie Morrill

WANDERER BOOKS

Published by Simon & Schuster, New York

Published by WANDERER BOOKS
A Simon & Schuster Division of
Gulf & Western Corporation
Simon & Schuster Building
1230 Avenue of the Americas
New York, New York 10020

Manufactured in the United States of America

10 9 8 7 6 5 4 3 2 1

Library of Congress Cataloging in Publication Data

Dixon, Franklin W
Mystery of smugglers cove.

(His Hardy boys mystery stories; 64)
SUMMARY: The art collector who suspects the Hardy boys of stealing one of his valuable paintings offers them a chance to prove their innocence by hiring them to find the painting and the real culprits.
[1. Mystery and detective stories] I. Title.
PZ7.D6444Myar [Fic] 80-15921

ISBN 0-671-41117-9
ISBN 0-671-41112-8 pbk.

Contents

1

Phony Proof

The phone rang shrilly. Frank and Joe Hardy looked up from the game of chess they were playing in the living room of their Bayport home.

"I wonder if it's for us," Frank said.

"We'll find out in a second," Joe replied. "Aunt Gertrude is picking it up in the hall."

Gertrude Hardy, who had been living with the family for quite some time, poked her head through the door a moment later. "Frank, Mr. Wester wants to talk to you."

"Mr. Wester?"

"You remember him—the retired banker. He's also a well-known art collector."

"Oh yes. Thanks, Aunty." Frank went into the

hall and picked up the receiver. "Mr. Wester, this is Frank Hardy."

"I want to see you and Joe," said the voice on the other end. "Can you come over here right away?"

"Sure thing. What's up?"

"I'm looking for a couple of crooks that you and your brother might be interested in. I want to see you two before I call the police!"

Wester hung up and Frank returned to the living room. He told Joe what the art collector had said.

"Wow!" Joe exclaimed. "Those thieves sound like they have him pretty worked up! Let's go!"

The boys flew out of the house. Eighteen-year-old Frank climbed behind the wheel of their yellow sports sedan. The dark-haired boy was a year older than his blond brother, who took the seat next to him. Both were known far beyond their hometown as excellent amateur detectives.

Frank drove along Elm Street to the main avenue and soon reached Raymond Wester's house on the outskirts of Bayport. It was almost a mansion, surrounded by acres of grass and huge trees.

Frank parked in the driveway. He and Joe noticed a woman glaring down at them from a second-floor window. She lifted her arm and they saw the gleam of a blade in her hand.

Joe gasped. "Looks like that lady's holding a dagger!"

"It sure does," Frank agreed. "I wonder what she's up to."

The woman turned away from the window and disappeared from sight. The Hardys got out of their car and went up the long front walk to the door. Joe reached for the bell, but before he had a chance to press it, the door opened a crack to reveal a gleaming blade!

Instinctively, they stepped back, and as the door swung wide open, they found themselves confronted by the woman from the second-floor window. She held a letter opener in one hand and a bunch of letters in the other.

"I saw you arrive," she said, "so I came down to let you in. I'm Mrs. Summers, the housekeeper. Mr. Wester is waiting for you."

She showed them through the hall into the art collector's study. The Hardys followed silently, embarrassed about mistaking the letter opener for a dagger.

Raymond Wester, a small man with white hair, was sitting behind a large oak desk. A number of paintings hung on the walls, except for an area over the fireplace where an oblong spot darker than the surrounding wall showed that a picture had recently been removed.

Wester motioned for Frank and Joe to take chairs in front of his desk.

"I suppose you're wondering why I asked you to come here," he began.

"That's right, sir," Frank admitted. "Except that you mentioned a couple of crooks."

Wester nodded. "They robbed me."

"What's missing?"

Wester pointed to the vacant space over the fireplace. "The painting that used to be there has disappeared. It was a very valuable portrait of Simón Bolívar. I suppose you know who Bolívar was."

Joe grinned. "We studied him in history class. He was the George Washington of South America. Knocked over the Spaniards the way Washington defeated the British."

"That's why they called him the Liberator," Frank added.

"You know your history," Wester complimented them. "Well, my portrait of Bolívar is gone. Vanished."

"When did it happen?" Frank inquired.

"Two weeks ago today. I was in Europe. When I arrived home this noon I found out it was gone."

"And you have no idea who might have taken it?" Frank asked.

"Well, let me tell you what happened. Before leaving on my trip last month, I ordered my secretary, Mark Morphy, to have the painting taken down and sent to my brother Harrison, who lives on Key Blanco in Florida. Harrison has always admired the portrait, so last month I agreed to give it to him."

"What method of transportation did you use?" Frank asked.

"The painting was too valuable to ship through the mails or a delivery service. I asked Morphy to hire two couriers to drive to Florida in a van. He was to go along and keep an eye on the picture at all times."

"Could they drive all the way to Key Blanco?" Joe inquired.

"No. Only to Key West. From there they were to hire a boat. Before leaving for Europe, I phoned Harrison and told him that the portrait would soon be on its way to him. However, when I returned today, he called and said it never arrived!"

"Did you inform the police?" Frank asked. "Perhaps there was an accident, and they might be able to locate the van between here and Florida."

Wester shook his head. "As I told you over the phone, I wanted to talk to you first. Anyway, if the van had had an accident, Morphy would have phoned me."

"You haven't heard from your secretary at all?"

"Not a word! I'm afraid he may have been kidnapped by those couriers. You know, I just can't believe he's involved in anything underhanded—"

"Did Morphy identify the couriers he hired?" Joe asked. "Did he leave their names?"

"Yes," Wester declared. "He also left a photograph of them."

"Good," Frank said. "That way we can go to Chief Collig at police headquarters and see if they're listed in his mug shot file."

"No need to go to all that trouble," Wester said dryly. "I think *you* can identify them."

"Why is that, Mr. Wester?" Joe asked, puzzled.

The retired banker took a photograph from a drawer and handed it to him. "Here!"

The young detectives stared at the picture and gaped in surprise. They were looking at a snapshot of themselves!

2

No Alibi!

"Morphy pulled a fast one on you, Mr. Wester," Joe finally said. "We never saw the painting or met the man."

"Besides, we're detectives, not couriers!" Frank pointed out emphatically.

"And not criminals either!" added Joe.

Wester appeared unconvinced. "You could be using your reputation for crime-fighting as a cover. Everyone in Bayport knows you've solved a lot of mysteries. Maybe you thought you wouldn't be suspected. That's a photo of you two, isn't it?"

"Sure," Frank admitted. "But it doesn't prove anything. I recognize the picture. It was shot by Andy Anderson of the *Bayport Times* during an interview. Morphy must have gone to the newspaper morgue and dug it out."

Wester shrugged. "If he did, he was still letting me know you and Joe were the couriers he hired. Where were you two weeks ago when my painting was stolen?"

"We were backpacking in Maine," Frank replied. "Followed the Appalachian Trail. It was great hiking—"

"That's what *you* say," Wester retorted suspiciously. "Did anyone see you?"

"No," Frank said. "I'm afraid we don't have that kind of alibi—we were alone!"

Wester was more suspicious than ever. "Why would Morphy name you if you weren't involved?"

"I guess he's trying to throw suspicion on us," Joe declared. "*He* seems like the number one suspect to me."

"But you might be in cahoots with him," Wester argued. "Maybe he ducked out with the portrait and left you to be the fall guys."

Frank and Joe stared at each other. It was the first time they had ever been accused of being crooks!

"Let's see if the real thief left a clue," Joe suggested. "We'll need to know all about the robbery. Is there someone who can tell us how it happened?"

"Mrs. Summers can," Wester said, "as if you don't know already."

Wester summoned the housekeeper, who entered the study and stared at the Hardys curiously. Her employer asked her to tell them what she knew about the missing portrait.

"When Mr. Wester was in Europe," she explained, "Mr. Morphy was in charge here. He told me he had orders to remove the painting and take it to Mr. Harrison Wester. He said he'd hire two couriers to drive to Key Blanco, and that he was leaving detailed information in the desk drawer."

"That's us," Joe put in. "Trouble is, Morphy never informed us of his scheme. Did he tell you anything else?"

"I had nothing to do with it!" the housekeeper snapped.

"Of course not," Frank said soothingly. "But please, what happened next, Mrs. Summers?"

"The following day Mr. Morphy gave the staff the day off. When we got back, the painting was gone."

"And Morphy was gone too?" Joe inquired.

"Yes," the housekeeper replied. "And I haven't seen him since."

Wester looked sternly at Frank and Joe. "I still think you may be in on it. And if you're not you'll just have to prove it!"

Joe had an idea. "What if Morphy only pretended to send the painting to Key Blanco, but actually hid it here?"

"May we search the house?" Frank added, catching on.

"Go ahead," the retired banker agreed. "Mrs. Summers will show you around. The portrait's about two by four feet. Should be easy to find if it's here."

The Hardys decided to search from the top down, and followed the housekeeper up to the attic. It was a dusty area covering the entire top floor. The only light in the dingy interior came from two small windows under the slanting roof.

A quick inspection convinced Frank and Joe that the missing portrait was not in the attic. Mrs. Summers led the way down to the next floor, where the servants' quarters were located. Nothing turned up, and they had no better luck on the two floors occupied by Wester.

"We've come up empty," Frank said in disgust.

"The basement's our last chance," Joe pointed out. "We'd better look—"

"Nothing's down there," Mrs. Summers interrupted. "I've already seen for myself."

"Our report has to be complete," Frank said diplomatically. "Do you mind if we take a quick look?"

The housekeeper shrugged and opened the cellar door. Everyone descended a flight of rickety stairs.

The basement had cinderblock walls and a cement floor. In one corner stood the furnace and water heater, and nearby, a workbench ran the length of one wall.

"Mr. Wester uses the bench to repair his paintings," the housekeeper explained.

In the darkest corner of the cellar, Joe spotted a heavy iron ring hanging from the wall. "What's this for?" he inquired.

"I don't know," Mrs. Summers snapped. "Now, can we go back up?"

"Wait a minute," Frank said. He was inspecting the iron ring. "It looks like a handle. Maybe there's a door in this wall."

Twisting the ring, he pulled hard on it. A section of cinder blocks moved to one side.

"It's a secret room!" Frank exclaimed. "Maybe the picture's in here!"

The boys went through the doorway. They found themselves in a small room, its back wall illuminated dimly by the basement light.

"Wow!" Joe said. "Who could have built this, and why?"

Frank shrugged. "Whoever built the house, I

suppose. Perhaps Mr. Wester knows what it was intended for."

The Hardys began to examine the wall closely. They were so absorbed in their task that they did not hear the door creak behind them. Suddenly it became darker in the room, and when they turned around, they realized that their light source from the basement was being cut off by the closing door.

Click! They heard the noise of the lock falling into place, then stood in complete darkness.

Frank leaped to the door and tried to open it. However, his palms flattened against unyielding cement blocks!

"Mrs. Summers!" he yelled. "Let us out!"

The housekeeper did not respond.

"She must hear us!" Joe said urgently. "The door isn't that thick!"

"Sh!" Frank said, trying to listen for Mrs. Summers's footsteps. There was nothing but silence!

Desperately, Frank felt around the door in the darkness to see if he could find a handle on their side. But his fingers touched only bare cinder blocks.

"Joe!" he exclaimed. "We're trapped!"

"Maybe there's another way out," Joe said encouragingly. He moved along the wall in the pitch darkness feeling for an outlet. Suddenly he stepped into empty air! His feet slipped out from

under him, and with a scream, he plunged into nothingness!

"Joe! Are you okay?" Frank called out, worried.

There was no reply. Frank stood stock-still, fighting a wave of panic that threatened to engulf him. Suddenly he remembered that he was carrying his pencil flashlight in the back pocket of his dungarees. He flicked it on and turned the beam in the direction of Joe's scream.

The light illuminated four wooden steps. Joe lay crumpled in a heap at the bottom!

Frank rushed to his brother's side and shook him gently. Joe opened his eyes, rubbed his head, then staggered to his feet.

"Next time I take a swan dive I'll make sure there's water in the pool," he said ruefully. "No harm done, though, except for a bump on my head."

Frank shone his flashlight up ahead and saw they were in a low, narrow passage only a few feet long. The floor slanted sharply upward.

"Maybe there's a door over there," he suggested. "Let's see."

He led the way forward, crouching down as the height of the passage decreased. But a quick inspection revealed that they were facing a blank wall at the end.

"That was our last chance," Frank lamented. "We're in a secret tunnel without an exit!"

Joe, exploring the low ceiling of the passage with his hands, came upon a large bolt fastened into a hasp.

"Wait a minute," he said. "This may be a way out!" Forcing the bolt back from its hasp, he pushed up. A small, square section of the ceiling opened outward, admitting daylight that caused the Hardys to blink and cover their eyes after their spell in the darkness. Clambering through the opening, they found themselves in a thick clump of bushes at the side of the house near the driveway.

Joe allowed the door to fall back into place. It became indistinguishable in a tangle of ivy.

"That's a neat way of hiding a secret passage," Frank noted. "Hey! What's this?" His foot had dislodged something in the ivy. He bent over and picked up a jackknife with a flat yellow plate on either side. One of them bore the letters *I.N.*

"The owner's initials!" Frank said excitedly, showing the knife to his brother. "Let's see if they fit anybody in the house."

Circling around to the front door, they rang the bell. Mrs. Summers answered and looked surprised to see them.

"That door in the basement fell shut all by itself," she explained. "I couldn't get it open, so I went looking for help. I was going to ask Mr. Wester to let you out, but he's on the phone."

"We found another exit," Frank informed her, then looked at her sharply. "Do the initials *I.N.* mean anything to you, Mrs. Summers?"

The housekeeper seemed startled, but shook her head. "No one here has those initials," she insisted.

"May we see Mr. Wester now?" Joe asked.

"Certainly." Mrs. Summers let them in, and the young detectives joined the art collector in his study. Wester hung up the phone as they walked through the door. He was taken aback when he heard about the secret passage in the basement. "I never knew it was there!" he declared. "But then, the house was built over a hundred years ago."

Frank had an idea. "Mr. Wester, if your secretary had anything to do with the theft of the painting, perhaps he stole other things, too. Have you noticed anything else missing?"

Wester shook his head but told Mrs. Summers to check. She came back shortly afterward, looking upset. "I didn't notice before," she said, "but the big silver pitchers have been taken out of the sideboard. Also the tall golden candlesticks."

"Someone, perhaps Morphy, has been robbing you blind," Joe commented.

"I just wonder why he didn't take more of the valuable paintings," Frank mused.

"He probably figured it would be too obvious," Joe reasoned.

Mrs. Summers nodded. "The pitchers and candlesticks were not openly displayed," she said. "I wouldn't have discovered that they were gone unless I'd checked."

"Did you find a clue while you were looking through the house?" Wester asked the boys.

"Just this," Frank said, showing him the jackknife.

The art collector did not recognize it, nor did he know the initials *I.N.* The Hardys then inspected the area above the fireplace where the Bolívar portrait had hung. A spot on the wall caught Frank's eye. He scrutinized it closely. "This is a pretty clear fingerprint," he declared. "Joe, do you want to get our kit from the trunk of the car?"

"I'll be right back," Joe said. He returned with a small box and sprinkled some powder over the spot. Then he photographed it with a small camera before lifting the print with a piece of special tape.

He turned to Wester. "If it's okay with you, I'll take another print from Morphy's room and we'll see if they match."

Wester told him to go ahead, and Joe left the study. Frank looked thoughtfully at the empty wall over the fireplace. "I wonder why whoever monkeyed with the picture didn't wear gloves."

Wester glowered at him. "Maybe you know as well as I do that the picture wire was twisted around the hook. The thief had to use his fingers to loosen it."

They discussed the mystery until Joe returned.

"I took a perfect print from the mirror Morphy used for shaving," the younger Hardy boy revealed. "Now we can have Chief Collig check both of them at police headquarters. Mr. Wester, we'll get back to you when we find out if they match. If they don't, the police might be able to figure out whose they are from their records."

Wester nodded. "While you're there, tell him my house has been robbed."

"We'll be glad to make the report for you," Frank assured him.

The art collector glared at him. "And don't forget to mention to the chief that it seems the main suspects are Frank and Joe Hardy!"

3

A Cry for Help

Frank and Joe stared at the art collector. Apparently he still believed they were guilty!

"We'll have to find Mark Morphy to clear ourselves," Frank said slowly. "What does he look like, Mr. Wester?"

Wester took another photograph out of his desk and handed it to Frank. "Here he is."

"Can you tell us anything else about him?" Frank went on. "Does he have a family and friends? Where did he live before he worked for you? Who recommended him to you?"

Wester shrugged. "He's been with me for a year. I hired him after his boss, an acquaintance of mine, passed away. I know nothing about his family or where he came from. He never mentioned it and I never asked."

The art collector could provide no further information about his secretary, so the boys left. On the way to police headquarters, they discussed the strange case.

"How do you like being called a crook?" Joe grumbled. "Wester is definitely suspicious of us. And why would he want to see us—alone—before telling the police?"

Frank nodded in disgust. "I don't trust that housekeeper of his. I bet she knew about the secret passage and locked us into that room on purpose."

Joe shrugged. "She said she wanted to call Wester but that he was on the phone. And we saw he was when we went into his study."

"She could have heard it ring and used it as an excuse," Frank said, unconvinced. He parked in front of Chief Collig's office, and the boys went inside to see their old friend, who had helped them on many of their cases.

The chief, a tall, burly man with ruddy cheeks, happened to be at his desk when they entered. "Boys, what can I do for you?" he asked in a friendly tone.

Joe placed the two fingerprints from the Wester

house in front of him. "We'd like to know if these match."

The chief squinted at the young detectives. "You're on another case, aren't you? Want to tell me about it?"

The Hardys described their visit to Raymond Wester's home and mentioned Wester's suspicion that *they* had had a hand in stealing his painting.

Collig whistled. "That puts you in the hot seat, doesn't it? Well, I'll see what I can do to get you off."

He led the way to the police crime laboratory and placed the two fingerprints under a dual microscope that he adjusted until the prints meshed at the edges. For a moment he peered intently through the eyepiece, then said, "They're not the same. See for yourselves."

Frank and Joe, who were skilled in the science of fingerprints, took turns at the microscope.

"Morphy's print is a loop," Joe noted. "The print from the wall is a double loop."

"They're from two different people," Frank agreed. "I wonder who the other one is."

"Let's see if we have anything on that," Collig offered. He went to his file of fingerprint cards and thumbed through them. After a few moments, he shook his head. "Nothing here. Your man is not a known local criminal. I'll wire the print to the FBI in Washington. Maybe they can identify it for you."

The chief added that he would look into the robbery at the Wester house. The Hardys drove home feeling reassured by Collig's support.

Their father, a New York City detective turned private investigator, had just arrived a few minutes earlier.

"I know Key Blanco," he said after hearing their story. "It's a center for smuggling in the Gulf of Mexico and the Caribbean. But Frank and Joe Hardy, alleged crooks! That's a new one in this family." He chuckled.

Mrs. Hardy frowned anxiously. "I think this case is too dangerous," she said in a worried tone.

Aunt Gertrude sniffed. "Laura, it happens all the time," she said. "Frank and Joe can find danger anywhere, even in the house of a respectable banker."

"Perhaps Wester's the crook," Joe said, grinning. "He may have robbed his own painting."

Gertrude Hardy shook her head in mock despair, then smiled. "Before you make any more clever deductions, young man, I have some chocolate cake in the kitchen for both of you." Despite her tart manner, she was very fond of her nephews and liked to spoil them with her excellent cooking.

Some time later, the phone rang. It was Chief Collig. "I have the FBI report on that second fingerprint," he told Joe, who had answered the call. "It belongs to a man named Ignaz Nitron. He once did time for burglary, and was last seen on Key Blanco."

"Key Blanco!" Joe exclaimed. "That's where Wester sent his painting! Thanks, Chief."

He hung up and reported the new development to the others.

"I've heard of Nitron," Fenton Hardy stated. "He's suspected of running a smuggling ring, but he's never been caught with the goods. Stealing the picture from the Wester home is the kind of thing he'd be involved in. Since it's a portrait of Simón Bolívar, he could easily find a wealthy buyer in Latin America."

"The initials on the jackknife must be his!" Frank said excitedly. "Perhaps he dropped the knife when he helped carry the picture through the secret passage to the driveway!"

Joe looked puzzled. "But what's a crook from Key Blanco doing in Bayport?"

"Maybe Harrison Wester talked about the portrait and Nitron heard about it," Frank theorized. "So he came to Bayport and grabbed it."

"Probably with the help of Morphy," Joe added. "And there might be a third crook. Morphy supposedly hired two couriers."

"Now don't jump to conclusions," his father warned. "Nitron, perhaps with the help of an accomplice, could have gotten rid of Morphy and planted your photograph in Wester's desk."

"I doubt it," Joe said. "Why would Morphy give the staff the day off unless he had something to hide?"

Mr. Hardy nodded slowly. "You have a point there. Anyway, it's a real puzzler. Your best bet is to go to Key Blanco and start investigating."

"We'll go underground and pose as smugglers," Frank suggested. "Hopefully we'll run into Nitron."

"And we'll keep an eye out for Morphy, too," Joe added.

Fenton Hardy approved of the plan. However, he warned the boys to be careful.

Just then the phone rang again. Frank picked it up. It was Raymond Wester, so the young detective motioned for Joe to pick up the extension.

"I'm at the Bayport Hotel!" Wester declared irritably. "Why aren't you boys here yet?"

"Why should we be, Mr. Wester?" Frank asked, perplexed.

"Because you asked me to meet you here!" the art collector snapped.

"But—we haven't talked to you since we left your home!" Frank protested. "We never mentioned the Bayport Hotel."

"Frank Hardy, you phoned about an hour ago," Wester accused him. "I expected you and Joe to be here. I thought you might have found my painting. I'm in room 707."

Frank was mystified. Instead of arguing the point over the telephone, he just said, "Okay, we'll be right over."

"Where did he get the idea you asked him to go to the hotel?" Joe wondered.

"Someone called him and imitated my voice," Frank said grimly. "Come on, we'll have to check this out!"

Both boys were rushing toward the door when Mr. Hardy called them back. "You'll have to look into this, I agree," the detective said. "But be very careful. You might be lured straight into a trap!"

4

Alligator Bait

Frank nodded thoughtfully. "You're right," he said. "If we're not back in half an hour, come after us, will you?"

"I sure will," his father promised, and the boys went out.

When they reached the Bayport Hotel, the desk clerk informed them that they were to call Mr. Wester instead of coming up to his room. Frank realized instantly that whoever had set them up wanted to be warned about their arrival.

"No need to," he told the clerk casually. "We just spoke to Mr. Wester a few minutes ago."

Quickly he and Joe went to the elevator. However, just before the doors closed, they caught a glimpse of the desk clerk dialing a number.

"He called the room anyway," Frank said tersely as they rode to the seventh floor. A few moments later they knocked on the door of room 707. The answer was a frightening groan. Joe opened the door and the boys gasped. Raymond Wester lay on the floor, his hands tied behind his back, while two men were escaping through the open window.

They wore stocking masks over their heads. Frank and Joe noticed that one of them was heavy-set and clad in checkered pants. The other was tall and muscular and just about to climb over the sill when he saw the boys. He grabbed a lamp from the bedside table and hurled it at them. Then he followed his partner down the fire escape.

The lamp hit Joe, who lost his balance and fell to the floor next to Wester.

"Frank, follow them!" he cried.

Frank circled around his brother and the art collector and rushed to the window. Quickly he swung his legs over the sill. Beneath him, he saw the fugitives rapidly descending the fire escape. They leaped to the ground and hurried to the parking lot around the side of the building.

Moments later, Frank reached the ground and ran after them. He heard the roar of an engine, then a car shot out of the lot and hurtled directly at him!

Frank's athletic ability enabled him to leap onto a heavy wire fence, find a toehold in its empty spaces, and cling desperately to its meshes with his fingers.

The car zoomed past him with inches to spare! He saw two faces disguised by stocking masks glaring at him from the front seat before the vehicle rolled through the exit and vanished down the street.

Frank jumped down to the ground. Wow! he thought. Any closer and I'd have been sitting in the front seat with those guys!

Shaken, he reentered the hotel lobby. The clerk stared at him in surprise. "Where're *you* coming from? I thought you—"

Frank did not reply. Instead, he walked right into the elevator and rode up to the seventh floor.

In Wester's room, he found his brother and the art collector sitting on the couch waiting for him.

"Those goons escaped in a car," Frank explained. "They almost ran me over. What happened to you, Mr. Wester?"

The retired banker looked uncomfortable and puzzled. "Well, I came to the hotel after I heard from you," he began. "Since you boys weren't here, I phoned to find out where you were. I had hardly put down the receiver when those two men came through the window."

"Did you recognize them?" Joe asked.

Wester shook his head. "Not with those masks on. They ordered me to tell you to leave when you called from the lobby, and threatened that my life wouldn't be worth a nickel if I didn't take you off the case."

Nervously he pulled out a handkerchief and wiped his brow. "Then the clerk called and said you were on your way up. The men did not expect this. They panicked, bound my hands, and took off through the window."

"Are you still suspicious of us?" Joe wanted to know.

"Why not?" Wester snapped. "You might want to get off the case and are using this setup at the hotel to make it look good. Tricked me into coming here and then sent those goons to manhandle me!"

"Then why did we come over here?" Joe demanded. "We could have stayed home and called you with an excuse instead of hotfooting it to the hotel and getting hit with a lamp."

"Or almost run over by a car," Frank added grimly.

Wester shrugged. "There's only one way you can make me stop suspecting you."

"What's that?"

"Stay on the case and solve it!" the retired banker boomed.

"We will," Frank promised. "We're headed for Key Blanco to begin our investigation."

"That's fine. Harrison has a house on a cliff on the east side of the island overlooking Smugglers Cove. I'll phone him and say that you're coming down."

"Thank you," Frank said. "We'll let you know our approximate arrival time."

Raymond Wester nodded, then left the hotel. Frank and Joe drove to their home on Elm Street. On the way, they discussed the incident.

"I don't get it," Joe said. "Why didn't those characters simply go to Wester's place and tell him to take us off the case? Why bother with this setup at the hotel?"

"To keep him suspicious of us," Frank pointed out. "Remember, he still thinks *I* called him to the hotel. Those crooks expect him to believe we arranged this whole thing because we really *are* guilty."

"I guess you're right."

When they arrived home, the boys took some books from their father's library into the living room and began to read about southern Florida. They discovered that Key Blanco was near Key West in the Gulf of Mexico.

"It was a pirates' lair in earlier times," Joe read from an encyclopedia, "and today is a center for smuggling despite the efforts of the U.S. Coast Guard to end this illegal traffic."

Frank was studying another volume. "It says here that Key Blanco has a lot of coves where smugglers run contraband ashore. That's why the coast guard has such a tough time catching them."

Suddenly a loud noise echoed outside. Startled, the Hardys wondered if it was a shot. They relaxed as the sound was followed by a series of backfires.

Frank grinned. "That's Chet with his jalopy."

Chet Morton was their best friend. A rotund youth who lived on a farm outside Bayport, he frequently accompanied the Hardys on their investigations. Although he would probably rate eating as his chief interest, the Hardy boys knew Chet would never let them down when they were in danger.

Joe went to the window and looked out. An old jalopy came up the street, backfiring at every turn of the wheel. Chet drove it like a cowpoke on a bucking bronco. His freckled face had a tense expression as he stopped with a jolt in front of the house and turned off the ignition.

Recognizing another friend beside Chet in the front seat, Joe said, "Biff's with him."

Biff Hooper was the star athlete of Bayport High. He knew how to use his fists when Frank and Joe were in a tight corner and needed help, since he, too, had been in on some of the Hardys' most dangerous cases.

Biff jumped out of the car and took a few steps with his hands on his hips, pretending to limp. Seeing Joe open the door, he called out, "Get me to a doctor! I've got a slipped disk from riding in this miserable heap!"

"Take another ride," Joe advised humorously. "Your disk will be jarred back into place."

Chet struggled to get his bulk past the steering wheel and eased himself onto the sidewalk. "Rave on!" he told his two friends. "This is the fastest car in Bayport. I could break the sound barrier with it."

"You'd break an axle before you were halfway down the track," Biff predicted.

Joe and the newcomers went inside and joined Frank in the living room.

Noticing the books about the Florida Keys on the table, Chet peered quizzically at the young detectives. "What gives? You guys going on a vacation?"

"I bet you're on another case," Biff declared.

"You're right," Frank said. "And it started right here in Bayport." Quickly he and his brother briefed his pals on the Wester mystery.

"Hey, can I come along?" Chet asked enthusiastically.

"Count me in too!" Biff added. He waved a fist in the air. "I'd like to get a few rounds with those crooks!"

"We're likely to run into a gang of smugglers," Joe warned.

"Smugglers, jugglers, they're all the same," Chet declared. "If it's a gang, you and Frank can use a couple of backstops."

The Hardys agreed that four would be better than two on Key Blanco, and that Chet and Biff would be welcome to go along if it was okay with their parents.

"We'll find out and get back to you as soon as we can!" Chet promised as he and Biff stormed out of the door. "Keep your fingers crossed!"

Frank and Joe went into the study to consult their father.

"I hope Chet and Biff will be able to go," Fenton Hardy said. "From what I hear, Key Blanco is a rough place, and you can use all the help you can get. Anyway, I'll alert the Key Blanco police that you boys will be posing as smugglers."

Later, Chet and Biff phoned to say they could go, and the four youths agreed to meet at the airport the following morning.

Their flight for Miami took off promptly. Their seats were located at the rear of the plane. The four friends relaxed and watched the states of the

East Coast fall behind as the plane thundered toward Florida.

Half an hour into the flight, Frank stood up to get a soda from the galley. When he returned, he put his drink down excitedly. "Hey! See those two guys sitting up front? One is tall and muscular, the other one fat. And he's wearing the same checkered pants as one of the heavies we ran into at the Bayport Hotel!"

Joe whistled. "Those pants looked so horrible on a shape like his that I can't believe this passenger is another man with the same bad taste!"

"What you're trying to say," Chet spoke up, "is that these people are the same men who tied up Raymond Wester?"

"Very likely!"

"I wish we could hear what they're saying," Joe said. "But if we go up there, they'll recognize us."

"They wouldn't recognize Biff and Chet," Frank declared. "How about it, fellows? Want to do a little detective work for us?"

Biff stood up with a grin. "There's nobody sitting behind them," he stated. "I'll see what I can do."

"Thanks, buddy."

Biff made a circle with his thumb and index finger to show he had everything under control. Then he strolled casually up the aisle and slipped into the empty seat. The passengers in front of him had their heads together and were talking in low voices.

"Bringing the Hardys into the case was a dumb idea," the fat man grumbled. "Morphy flubbed it when he left that photograph and said they were the couriers he hired to take the painting to Key Blanco."

"He thought it would fool everybody," the tall man said with a shrug. "Morphy figured that Raymond Wester would sic the police on the Hardys. Unfortunately, he hired them instead!"

The fat man gritted his teeth. "And you know, Tom, our trick to force him into taking those kids off the case didn't work either."

"You're right. Instead of giving up, they'll probably stick to this assignment like a couple of bulldogs. They have a reputation for never giving up. What if they find out me and Nitron took the picture?"

"They might find out more than that! Suppose they get wise to the whole smuggling operation? I still say we shoulda finished 'em off in Bayport. Those scare tactics the chief wanted us to use were strictly for the birds!"

Tom sighed. "We gotta follow orders. And if the Hardys catch up with us, we'll toss 'em to the alligators!"

5

Alley Ambush

Biff clenched his fists on hearing the evil remark. That's what you think! he thought angrily while listening closely to the continued conversation.

"The sooner we knock off the Hardys, the better I'd like it," the fat man was saying.

"Here's what we'll do, Fatso, if the Hardys give us a hard time," Tom proposed. "We'll kidnap 'em and take 'em to—"

Biff leaned forward to hear better. Tom noticed the movement out of the corner of his eye and suddenly whirled around to confront him!

Just then the plane shuddered in a downdraft and tilted over on its nose. Biff was thrown against the seat in front of him when the plane dipped to one side in the violence of its descent. The next moment he tumbled into the aisle!

Fatso and Tom hit the wall separating them from the galley. There were confused shouts from the other passengers as the plane hurtled toward the ground.

"We're gonna crash!" Fatso yelled in terror.

Then the pilot regained control of the craft. The plane leveled out, and zoomed upward again to a safe altitude. The travelers calmed down and the two men fell back into their seats with sighs of relief.

Biff scrambled to his feet as Tom stared at him suspiciously.

"Kid, were you eavesdropping on us?" the tall man growled.

"I lost my balance when the plane started to go down," Biff replied apologetically. "I did a nose dive into the seat behind you and then got thrown out into the aisle. I didn't hear a word you said."

"Well, you better go back to your seat and stay there," Tom warned him.

"And use your seat belt," Fatso added. "That way you'll stay put instead of draping yourself all over us!"

Biff grinned as if to say he was embarrassed by the accident. He made his way down the aisle and joined his friends. Quickly he reported what he had heard the two men say.

"They're the guys from the hotel all right," Frank said. "And they're smugglers! How do you like that?"

"The tall guy, Tom, was in on the picture heist," Chet noted. "Apparently he and Nitron were the couriers Morphy hired."

"And Morphy's definitely their accomplice," Joe said.

"I wonder who the chief is," Chet said. "Must be the top man on the smugglers' totem pole."

Frank was puzzled. "But why did they talk about alligators? There aren't any 'gators on Key Blanco. They're in the Everglades."

"Let's shadow these guys when we arrive in Miami," Joe suggested. "They might lead us to the rest of the gang."

Suddenly Chet looked up and saw the two men advancing toward them along the aisle.

"Frank and Joe, watch out!" he hissed.

Catching on instantly, the Hardys took defensive measures. Joe hastily picked up a newspaper he had been reading and handed part of it to his brother. They put the pages over their faces and pretended to be asleep.

The men came closer and stopped at the line of

seats occupied by the boys from Bayport. Biff got ready for action by clenching his hands into a pair of fists and was about to tell the Hardys that a free-for-all was coming. Just then Tom called to a flight attendant.

"Where're the pillows for the seats up front?"

"Yeah, how do you expect us to sleep?" Fatso barked.

The pretty, dark-haired woman smiled soothingly. "I'll bring you a couple of pillows right away."

The two men retired to their seats and the boys looked after them with relieved grins. "The coast is clear," Biff announced, and Frank and Joe dropped the newspaper.

"They didn't see you," Chet declared. "You ducked under those pages just in time."

Joe looked at the section he had been using and chuckled. "What do you know. The sports page. Joe Hardy was saved by the baseball scores."

Suddenly Chet's eyes lit up. "I see the chow coming, fellows! Get ready for the feast!"

The flight attendant pushed a cart from the galley up to where they were sitting and handed them trays with fruit juice, chicken, vegetables, and an apple tart.

The other three began to eat in a leisurely manner, but Chet pitched in with great gusto. In rapid succession the contents of his tray disappeared. After he downed the last piece of apple tart, he leaned back blissfully in his chair, patted his stomach, closed his eyes, and went to sleep.

Frank chuckled. "Chet and food always go together."

"Like ham and eggs," Biff agreed.

The plane crossed the Florida border and soon the Tamiami Trail became visible snaking its way across the state.

When they landed in Miami, the Hardys again took refuge behind the newspaper pages, since the two smugglers started for the rear exit. The boys waited till Tom and Fatso had filed past, then brought up the end of the line where they could watch the men without being noticed.

The pair went through the lobby to a rent-a-car desk. As they were making arrangements for a car, Frank did the same at the counter of another company. Starting their car at a safe distance, the young detectives were able to follow the smugglers as they pulled away from the terminal in a blue compact.

Biff drove, with Chet beside him. Frank and Joe occupied the rear seat to avoid being seen.

"I have a hunch the smugglers are going to Key Blanco, too," Frank said as the lead car headed south through Miami Springs toward Coral Gables.

"Good," Joe said. "This way it's no detour for us. All we have to do is follow them."

"That's easier said than done," Biff grumbled. "This traffic's terrible."

He maneuvered their car through Coral Gables, keeping the blue compact in view but not getting close enough to be seen and arouse suspicion.

At a major intersection, the light turned amber. The blue compact picked up speed and raced through. Biff tried to follow, but the signal changed to red and he was forced to slam on the brakes. The smugglers vanished on the other side of the light!

"Oh, rats. We've lost them," Biff said, disappointed. "What do we do now?"

"Forget them," Chet suggested. "Who needs them anyway? I'll solve the case once we get to Key Blanco!"

His companions, who were used to Chet's boastfulness, laughed, then decided to take his advice since they had no alternative. They left South Miami, Kendall, and Perrine behind and paused for a snack at a fast-food restaurant in Cutler Ridge. Then they rolled south again along the main route, making good time until they were near Homestead.

Suddenly the blue compact came into view up ahead.

"There they are!" Biff cried out. "We've caught up with them."

"Don't lose them again," Joe urged.

Biff stepped on the gas and drew closer to the smugglers than he had before. "I'll have to stick to them," he said. "But it'll be dark soon, so they probably won't spot us that easily."

As the two cars whizzed along the highway, Frank said, "I wonder why they're in such a hurry!"

"I have a feeling we'll find out," Chet predicted.

There was no one between the two vehicles as they entered Homestead. The compact took a route to the center of town. Biff kept up the pursuit.

Suddenly the blue car swerved sharply to the right, turned a corner, and was lost to sight. It happened so quickly that Biff nearly drove past the corner. He hit the brakes and wrenched the wheel to the right as hard as he could, his tires squealing as he made the turn.

They found themselves in a dark alley with sheer brick walls on both sides. A flashlight blinking in the middle of the road forced Biff to a jolting stop. The boys could see the tail lights of another car parked about twenty yards ahead of them.

The flashlight moved and its beam hit Biff in the eyes before swinging over to Chet. Out of the pitch blackness, Tom's voice snarled at Biff:

"Kid, you've tailed us far enough! This is the end of the chase for you and that fat kid next to you!"

6

A Surprising Clue

"It's an ambush!" Joe whispered to Frank hoarsely. "But he hasn't seen us. Duck!"

The Hardys hit the floor just before the beam of the flashlight played over the rear seat. Finding it empty, Tom turned back to Biff and Chet.

"We saw you kids tailing us on the highway," he snarled. "So we set a little trap for you, and you ran right into it. Now, what are you up to?"

Realizing they were dealing with dangerous men, Biff decided to try to talk his way out of the ambush.

"We weren't tailing you," he replied innocently. "Matter of fact, we're on our way to the Florida Keys for a little vacation. You see, my aunt lives there and she invited us to stay with her for a couple of weeks."

Chet caught on instantly. "We were talking about the Everglades and I guess my friend didn't pay much attention to the road. So he made the wrong turn into the alley. I hear the Everglades are really nice. Lots of alligators."

Tom coughed nervously. "What do you know about alligators?" he demanded.

"Oh, some guys wrestle them," Chet replied with a silly grin. "That's what I'd like to do. I'd love to make the alligator wrestling team."

"Very funny," Tom scoffed.

Biff rambled on. "You might be caught by poachers," he said to Chet. "There's lots of those in the Everglades, too!"

"Poachers?" Tom asked sharply.

"Sure. They shoot 'gators and sell their skins. I read about them in a magazine. They—"

"That's enough!" Tom exploded. "Now get out of the car!"

Biff hesitated, but Chet nudged him in the ribs with his elbow. "Don't take any chances!" the chubby boy urged in an undertone. "That guy might have a gun!"

He got out of the passenger seat and walked around to where Biff emerged from behind the wheel. The two youths wondered what would happen next. Frank and Joe, meanwhile, waited in the back of the car with bated breath.

"We're taking you down the shore for a swim!" Tom growled savagely at Biff and Chet. "A permanent one—underwater!"

"But—we didn't do anything!" Chet quavered.

"Shut up and get in that car over there, pronto!"

By now it was too dark to see, but a metallic click told the boys that the man was, indeed, armed, and that he had just flipped the safety catch of his gun. They had no choice but to obey! Nervously they started for the blue compact, with their captor close behind.

"We can't let this guy kidnap Chet and Biff!" Joe whispered to Frank.

"You bet we can't!" Frank agreed. "Come on!" He silently slid out of the car, with Joe right behind him. Luckily Biff had left the door half open.

Stealthily, the Hardys crept up on Tom and then tackled him from behind. Chet and Biff heard the commotion, whirled around, and joined in the fray.

A violent struggle erupted. Tom's gun clattered onto the cobblestones as Frank grabbed his wrist. The boys had just about overpowered him when Fatso realized that his companion was in trouble.

Quickly he put the blue compact into reverse and careened down the alley.

"Look out!" Frank yelled. "He's headed straight for us!"

The four boys jumped to one side and flattened themselves against the brick wall. Tom leaped in the opposite direction, waving furiously for Fatso to help him.

The compact jammed to a stop a few feet from the boys. Tom opened the door and, with the interior light on momentarily, the boys saw Fatso glaring at them evilly.

"Let's get out of here!" Tom grated. "There's four of 'em, not just two!"

The door slammed shut and Fatso stepped on the gas. Leaving a cloud of dust behind, the criminals sped through the alley.

Coughing, the four Bayport youths walked toward their own car and watched the compact's back lights moving away from them. The next moment, they disappeared altogether.

"There they go around the corner," Biff grumbled. "There's no way we can catch them now!"

Frank nodded. "It's too bad—" he started to say, when his foot hit something that skidded on the cobblestones with a metallic ring. He felt in the darkness until his fingers closed around the gun Tom had dropped during the struggle. He carried the weapon to the car and examined it in the interior light, while the others looked on. Joe took the Hardys' fingerprint kit from his bag and dusted the butt lightly with powder, hoping to find a print. But it was to no avail.

"Tom must have worn gloves," Joe said.

Biff shuddered, "A real pro. Lucky we didn't give him a hard time when he was pointing that gun at us."

"Well, it's a clue," Joe observed.

"We'll have it checked out at police headquarters," Frank agreed. "Maybe they can identify the owner."

"I vote we do it in the morning," Chet declared. "First we should get some rest. I'm beat!"

The others agreed and drove to the next motel, where they took a room for the night. Before going to sleep, they discussed their experience in the alley.

"I wonder why that guy got so worked up when Biff talked about poachers," Chet said. "It was just a joke."

Frank shrugged. "Who knows? Anyway, the men now know that we're on to them. Our cover's blown already."

"What are we going to do?" Chet asked.

"We'll think of something," Frank declared. "Let's sleep on it."

That night, Chet dreamed about being chased by alligators. He was in a swamp in the Everglades, running at top speed while the giant lizards came after him with open jaws. Then he tripped and fell. In a flash, the vicious alligators were upon him.

With a choked scream, Chet woke up. It was already daylight. He shook his head and shuddered, blinked his eyes a few times, then got out of bed. His friends were already dressing.

After breakfast, they all drove to police headquarters. Frank and Joe went in while Chet and Biff stayed in the car.

A lieutenant received the Hardys in his office. "I've heard about your father's detective work, and about the crimes you boys have solved," he said with a smile. "What's on your mind?"

Frank drew the gun from his pocket and handed it to him. The officer inspected it closely. After learning how Frank had obtained the weapon, he went to his file of licensed gun owners in Florida and slowly flipped through it.

"You're in luck," he said finally, pulling out a card. He handed it to the Hardys.

Frank and Joe stared in amazement.

"Why, it's registered to Harrison Wester of Key Blanco!" Frank cried out.

"He's the brother of the man who hired us to

find a missing painting," Joe explained and briefly outlined their case to the lieutenant.

"We'll take the gun to Mr. Wester," he added. "It must have been stolen from him."

The officer nodded. "Harrison Wester has an excellent reputation. But I cannot return the gun unless he claims it as missing. Please tell him to call me when you get there."

"We sure will," Frank promised, then the Hardys left. They joined their friends and soon the group was rolling down Route 1 with Joe at the wheel and Frank following directions on the map.

"I wonder if Mr. Wester missed the gun," Chet spoke up. "Maybe he knows those guys we tangled with."

"They could have bought it on the black market," Frank observed.

"You mean, somebody else stole the gun from Mr. Wester and then sold it?"

Frank nodded. "Lots of crooks do that."

Joe stepped on the gas and the car picked up speed as they approached the southern tip of Florida.

"Anyway," he said, "the gun's another clue leading to Key Blanco. Trouble is, we don't know where to go from there. This case is certainly a mystery."

"Dangerous too, judging by our last encounter with Tom and Fatso," Biff added.

"If there's more danger, count me out!" said Chet hastily.

Joe chuckled. "Come on. We need you. We know you're the bravest soul in Bayport!"

Chet grinned. "Okay, I'll tackle the crooks," he promised. "But you'd better be there to back me up. I can't take on more than five at a time."

Chet's joke made the others laugh. They continued in high spirits until they reached a long bridge extending from the Florida mainland out over the water.

"Where are we now?" Biff asked.

"We're crossing the Intracoastal Waterway," Frank told him. "Key Largo's straight ahead. It's the longest of the Florida Keys, by the way."

Joe turned south on the Overseas Highway linking the islands of the chain to one another. The boys sped from one key to the next, enjoying the sunlight, the warm air, and the blue-green water on either side.

"The Overseas Highway is the longest ocean-going highway in the world," Joe commented. "So says our encyclopedia."

"Great place for scuba diving," Chet said, looking out over the wide expanse of water.

"We came here to solve a case, not for a vacation," Joe reminded him.

"We-e-l-ll," Chet drawled, "couldn't we go diving *after* we catch the crooks?"

Frank chuckled. "Maybe."

U.S. Navy ships were coursing through the sea leaving trails of foaming white water in their wake. Navy planes roared overhead, and a group of Phantom jets zoomed down so low it seemed they might crash. The thunder of their engines sounded deafening in the car. On cue, the pilots maneuvered their craft up in one great arc, then raced into the distance until they were lost in the bright, blue sky.

The boys crossed the bridge into Key West, the last of the islands linked by the Overseas Highway. Slowly they drove down narrow streets between rows of closely packed houses. Near the southern end, they noticed a sign saying KEY WEST NAVAL BASE.

Just then, Chet spotted a blue compact moving along a side street. "Hey!" he cried excitedly. "There're the smugglers!"

7

Stealthy Figures in the Night

"Where?" Joe asked.

"Around the corner!" Chet pointed to where he had seen the blue compact.

Joe quickly turned up the side street, and the boys noticed the car heading into a parking lot.

Under Chet's prodding, Joe followed and stopped near the compact. Then the chubby boy opened the door.

"Wait a minute!" Frank exclaimed suddenly, after taking a closer look at the car they had just chased. But Chet was already outside and rushing up to the blue compact. His fists were raised as he stopped in front of the driver's door.

It opened and a naval officer climbed out!

Chet's eyes grew as round as saucers and his mouth fell open. Embarrassed, he dropped his hands to his sides.

"Is there something you want?" the officer inquired.

Chet blushed. "Er-r-r, no sir," he stammered. "I'm afraid I mistook you for someone else."

The officer shrugged and walked off in the direction of the Naval Base.

Chet rejoined his companions, his face red as a beet.

"You should have waited when I told you to," Frank said. "I noticed the license plate. It's not the same as the one we're looking for."

Chet nodded lamely. "Next time I'll let *you* guys chase the crooks."

The boys continued through Key West, found a rent-a-car lot, and turned in their car.

"How do we get to Key Blanco?" Joe asked the attendant.

"Ferry. Three blocks east, then go left down to the water. The boat'll drop you at Blanco City."

At the dock, the Bayporters found they were just in time for the next ferry. Quickly they bought tickets and went aboard. About twenty other passengers were standing at the rail or sitting on long wooden benches.

The ferry pulled away from its slip and headed

into open water. Key West dropped out of sight and the vessel pushed on through waves that grew heavier in a rising wind.

The boys went inside the main-deck cabin and stood by a window away from other passengers. As they discussed the Wester case in undertones, a tropical storm began to develop, causing the ferry to plunge up and down. Huge waves broke over the bow and sent clouds of spray splashing against the windows.

Chet turned pale and shuddered every time the ferry hit a wave. Looking queasy, he placed one hand on his belt buckle and the other against the windowsill in an effort to steady himself.

"I think I'll sit this one out," he croaked.

Staggering over to a row of empty seats, he lay down and after a few minutes was sound asleep. A loud, rhythmical sound came from his corner.

"Chet's snoring." Frank laughed. "Let's not forget to take him along when we arrive!"

But their friend awoke on his own just as the boat was docking in Blanco City. The storm had subsided and Chet hurried to the head of the passenger line so he could be first ashore. The Hardys and Biff followed.

Frank asked the ticket attendant how to get to Smugglers Cove.

"One mile north," the man replied. "Can't miss

it. There's a big house on the cliff, the Wester place. You can walk along the beach."

The four boys set out in a group, but Chet soon fell behind. He struggled to keep his footing in the sand. Sweat ran down his face, and he began to puff.

"This is murder," he complained.

"Cheer up," Frank replied. "We're almost there."

Joe pointed to a house on a cliff up ahead. "That must be the Wester place."

Steps made of heavy wooden logs led to the top of the steep incline. They climbed up and found themselves on a flagstone patio at the rear of the big house. From there they could see how Smugglers Cove was formed by a narrow beach that ran in an arc at the base of the cliff from one sandy headland to another.

Walking around to the front door, the boys noticed that the house faced a mass of mangrove trees and other tropical vegetation.

Frank rang the doorbell. A maid led them into the living room, where Harrison Wester was inspecting a row of paintings on the wall. He was a medium-sized man with white hair, who limped badly, supporting himself with a stout cane.

"I injured my leg scuba diving," he explained. "That's why I don't get around too well. My brother Raymond said the two Hardy boys would be coming down here. I see four of you."

"Reinforcements, Mr. Wester," Frank said. "Chet Morton and Biff Hooper. I hope you don't mind."

"Of course not. I've got plenty of room," Wester replied with a chuckle. "As long as you find my picture. When Raymond phoned from Bayport to say the Bolívar portrait would be on its way in the care of two couriers, I couldn't wait for it to arrive. But it never did, nor did the couriers. They must have stolen it."

"Do you think the picture ever reached Key Blanco?" Joe asked.

Wester shrugged. "It's possible. This island is notorious for smuggling, and the best thing for the thieves to do would be to ship the portrait from here to a place where it could be sold. It has probably left Key Blanco already, if it was, indeed, brought here. Anyway, I hope you boys can find it again!"

"We have a good clue," Joe revealed. "One thief left his fingerprint in Bayport when he took the picture from the wall. His name is Ignaz Nitron. Do you know him, by any chance?"

Wester shook his head. "Never heard of him."

"There's another clue," Frank put in. "We found your gun in Homestead."

Wester looked startled. "What do you mean, my gun?"

Frank explained about Tom, the tall man who had been Nitron's accomplice in stealing the picture. He described how Tom and Fatso had been sent to Bayport to get the Hardys off the case, how they had jumped Raymond Wester at the Bayport Hotel, and how they had been shadowed by the boys from Miami to Homestead, where Tom had dropped the gun during their struggle in the alley.

"We took it to police headquarters, and they informed us that the weapon was registered in your name, sir," the young detective concluded.

Wester, looking bewildered, checked the bottom drawer of his desk, which proved empty. "I don't know anything about these men," he declared. "And I have no idea how they got my gun. I haven't missed it because I haven't done any target practice in the last few weeks, and that's all I use it for. Otherwise it stays here," he said motioning to the drawer. "I can't imagine who could have stolen it!"

"What about Mark Morphy?" Chet spoke up.

"My brother's secretary? No way."

"He's an accomplice of the thieves," Biff pointed out. "Tom mentioned that fact to Fatso on the plane."

"And Morphy hasn't been seen since the disappearance of the picture," Joe added.

Wester was flabbergasted. "This is all news to me!" he said, greatly disturbed. "I never would've believed it of Mark Morphy. My, you can't trust anybody these days!"

"This is Smugglers Cove," Chet said. "Do you think the crooks are operating out of here?"

"Hardly, Chet," Wester replied. "Smugglers Cove was known for that kind of thing in the days of piracy. Nowadays no one could get away with transferring contraband down there. They'd be spotted from this house."

Chet seemed disappointed.

"The island, however, is still known for illegal activities," Wester continued, noticing the look on Chet's face. "But the smuggling goes on in areas far away from where people live."

"We'll have to check those out," Chet decided.

Wester nodded. "I hope you're successful," he said. "Do you see that landscape over the fireplace? It's the same size as the Bolívar portrait. That's why I intend to hang them side by side. That is, if you find the Bolívar portrait for me. In fact, I can just see it hanging there right now," Wester added, chuckling quietly.

"We'll find it," Joe vowed.

Wester showed the four around the house, balancing himself on his cane, and assigned them rooms on the second floor. "Make yourselves at home," he offered. "I'll see you at dinner. After that, I'll leave you to the mystery of the missing picture."

He limped downstairs while his guests inspected their accommodations, then gathered in Frank's room to discuss a plan of action.

"Let's keep our moves secret," Frank warned. "We'll go underground as smugglers without telling Mr. Wester, because he might spill the beans inadvertently. The less he's involved, the better."

"That should be no problem," Joe said. "All he wants us to do is find his picture. He doesn't care how we do it."

The others agreed. Just then the dinner bell rang, and the boys joined Mr. Wester in the dining room. Hungry after their long journey, they dug into the chicken and dumplings with gusto.

"I suggest you start your investigation in Blanco City," Wester announced. "You might find a clue there."

"Good idea," Frank said.

"Well, you know more about detective work than I do," Wester went on. "Make this house your headquarters. There are snacks in the refrigerator if you get hungry, and you can use the stereo in the living room if you want to."

He stood up from the table and limped into his study. The boys strolled into the living room and listened to country music until bedtime. Then they retired to their rooms and went to sleep.

In the middle of the night Frank suddenly woke up at the sound of footsteps in the hall. Floorboards creaked as someone moved stealthily past his room. Frank got out of bed and quietly opened the door. He peered into the hall.

A figure was tiptoeing toward the stairs!

I'd better see what this guy's up to, Frank thought. *Must be a burglar.* Silently he followed as the figure descended and went into the living room.

"Maybe he's after the pictures on the walls," Frank muttered to himself. But the figure continued on through the dining room into the kitchen.

He's stolen what he came for and is about to escape through the back door! went through Frank's mind. *I must head him off!*

In a flash, the young detective raced to the rear door and turned the key in the lock. Then he snapped on the light. The stealthy figure was standing next to the refrigerator.

"Chet!" Frank exclaimed.

Chet grinned. "I'm after a snack, like Mr. Wester said. I guess that's why you followed me. You want one, too!"

"A snack!" Frank cried indignantly. "I thought you were a thief sneaking through the house in the dark like that!"

Chet laughed. "Do I look like a thief?"

"Why not? There are fat thieves, you know."

"Come on! I'm not fat. Only well-nourished."

"Chet," Frank said in exasperation, "it's past three o'clock in the morning. I'm not going to argue about your physique. I just wish I hadn't woken up!"

Chet had taken two slices of pie out of the refrigerator and put them on plates. "Here, have some. It'll make you feel better."

Frank couldn't help but laugh. "Morton's remedy for all occasions. Thanks."

When they were finished, the boys cleaned up and went back to bed. Some time later Frank was again woken by footsteps in the hall. I wonder if that's what Chet does at home, the Hardy boy thought grumpily, get up every couple of hours to eat! He did not feel like leaving his bed, but his detective instinct would not let him go back to sleep. Perhaps it was not Chet, after all. He rose and opened the door. The stealthy figure was already at the stairs.

Frank followed quietly so as not to wake anyone else. He was about to go directly to the kitchen to head Chet off at the refrigerator, when he saw the figure go to the front door and open it.

The sun had just risen and the morning light afforded Frank a clear view of the stranger. "Hey!" the boy called out. "Wait a minute!"

The intruder turned for a moment, then rushed out the door, slamming it behind him.

"Mark Morphy!" Frank gasped.

8

Clever Disguise

For a moment the closed door delayed Frank's pursuit. When he emerged from the house, Morphy was already heading toward the steps to the beach. Frank ran after him as fast as he could and chased the man down to Smugglers Cove, where Morphy dashed toward an outboard motorboat drawn up on the sand. Being barefoot gave Frank an advantage. He quickly cut the distance between them, and finally grabbed Morphy near the water's edge.

The two fell down and rolled over and over in a wild wrestling match. Morphy broke free and bounded to his feet, only to be tripped by Frank, who pounced on him again. They fought desperately until suddenly Morphy scooped up a handful of sand and threw it into Frank's face!

Blinded, the young detective wiped his tearing eyes. He regained sight in time to see Morphy push the outboard into the water, jump aboard, and start the engine. The boat chugged away from shore, turned left around an outcropping of rock, and disappeared, its sound dying away in the distance.

Frank was furious. With burning eyes, he stared after the intruder, angry at himself for not catching the man. Then he went back to the house and washed the rest of the sand from his face in the shower. No one was up yet except for the household help. Frank dressed and went into the living room, trying to calm himself by looking at magazines.

When Wester and his friends came down for breakfast, Frank briefed them about what had happened. Wester looked shocked. "Morphy's never been here before! I've only seen him in Raymond's home in Bayport. Are you positive it was him?"

"Your brother showed us a picture. There is no doubt in my mind that he was the man I chased out of this house this morning."

"But why would he come here?"

"He knows you have a number of valuable paintings," Joe put in. "Perhaps he came to steal another one."

"But what was he doing upstairs?" Chet asked.

"He may have been looking for my Degas!" Wester said excitedly. "It's the most valuable painting I own! For the longest time I had it in the dining room, then I moved it to my bedroom because I like to look at it before I go to sleep."

"Did Morphy know about this picture?" Frank asked.

"It's quite possible Raymond mentioned it when he talked about our interest in art," Wester replied. "Well! I'll leave it to you boys to investigate—Chet, I hear you had some difficulty walking along the beach from Blanco City. You'll be pleased to know there's an easier path along the top of the cliff."

"Aren't you going to call the police about the Morphy incident?" Frank inquired.

Wester hesitated for a moment. "I don't see what they can do unless something's missing. I'll check. Meanwhile, I'm counting on you to find out exactly what's going on." With that, he limped back into his study.

The boys finished their breakfast, then set out for Blanco City. On the way, they talked about going underground and getting in touch with the smugglers.

"Let's disguise ourselves as sailors," Frank suggested.

"Good idea," Joe said. "That way we can snoop around the waterfront where smugglers hang out without being suspected."

"What about our faces?" Chet asked. "Tom and Fatso'll recognize us if we run into them!"

"That occurred to me," Frank replied. "While I was in the living room alone this morning, I checked the telephone book. There's a place on Market Street that sells theatrical props and make-up."

Chet grinned. "Good thinking!"

"We can fix your face so your own mother wouldn't recognize you," Frank added. "It's just too bad we can't change your shape!"

Chet shot his friend a sideways glance. "So? There're fat sailors, you know!"

Frank laughed. "I thought the word was well-nourished!"

At an Army-Navy store the boys bought seamen's work clothes and duffel bags in which they stuffed their regular pants, shirts, and shoes. Then they went to the shop on Market Street and picked out some instant hair color, beards, and a mustache for Chet. They completed their disguise in a deserted section of a park, then turned down toward the waterfront, making sure they were not being followed.

Ships at the docks were being loaded and unloaded by longshoremen, while businessmen were listing cargoes. Sailors were strolling ashore on leave, and visitors walked around, watching the picturesque scene.

"Act natural," Frank warned his companions. "Our story is, we've got a valuable cargo and are looking for a buyer, okay?"

"We'll talk about it," Joe added, "and just hope someone'll hear us and want to make a deal."

"When we get a bite," Biff suggested, "let's say we have electronic calculators to sell. I hear that's the hottest thing going right now."

The four coordinated their strategy and then mingled with the buzz of activity on the waterfront. They strolled along talking loudly about the valuable cargo they had to sell. A number of sailors, longshoremen, and businessmen turned to listen, but no one said anything.

Finally the boys halted at the end of the harbor. They found a bench, dropped their duffel bags, and sat down to discuss their next move.

"Let's try the coffee shops and restaurants," Frank proposed. "Places where sailors hang out when they're ashore."

The others agreed, but as they were about to move, Joe heard a rustling in the bushes behind them. Whirling around, he saw a man staring at them through the branches.

The stranger realized he had been seen and let the twigs snap back into place. Joe leaped up and rushed through the bushes, followed by the others.

The fugitive hurried across a footpath beyond the dock area. Reaching the nearest building, a restaurant, he ran through the back door. Joe followed, brushing between the stoves and carving blocks, scaring the chef and his cooks who were preparing meals.

The stranger careened through the swinging door into the dining room. He raced between the tables, pushed the headwaiter to one side, and went through the revolving door. He passed the front window and vanished.

Joe came next, but by now the headwaiter stood in his path with upraised hands. Frank, Chet, and Biff stopped behind Joe.

"Just what do you think you're doing?" the man demanded.

"We're chasing a suspect," Joe explained.

The headwaiter turned pale. "Did he take the cash in the till?"

"Not yet, but he might if we don't catch him. He'll get away if you don't let us through!" Joe said desperately.

The man stepped to one side. "Go ahead! If he's taken any of the silver, I'll bring charges against him!"

The boys pushed out onto the sidewalk and looked down the street. But the eavesdropper was nowhere in sight.

"What rotten luck!" Joe lamented. "Who do you think he was?"

Frank shrugged. "Maybe he heard us talking before and was curious."

"If he wanted to make a deal, he wouldn't have taken off," Biff pointed out.

"True," Frank admitted. "But from what I could see, he was a very straight-looking guy. Had a camera around his neck. Perhaps a young reporter after a big story. When we all jumped up and tried to get him, he scrammed."

Joe nodded. "I don't believe Tom, Fatso, or Morphy would recognize us in these outfits. So they didn't send him to spy on us."

"And we weren't followed after we put on our beards and stuff," Chet added.

They returned to the bench on the waterfront and were about to pick up their duffel bags when they heard another noise in the bushes.

"Sh!" Frank whispered. "There he is again. This time let's split up and see if we can trap him between us."

Quickly Biff and Chet circled around the clump of bushes. When they were lost to view, Frank and Joe walked straight toward the point from where the noise had come. Just then a figure became visible behind some branches. The four friends converged on the stranger in a flash and pinned him to the ground.

"All right, smarty!" Chet grated. "We've got you this time!"

"Who's Smarty?" their captive asked. Just then the boys realized that he was not the man who had eavesdropped on them before.

"Someone spied on us a few minutes ago. We thought you were the same guy," Frank explained.

"Well, I'm not. I wanted to talk to you about the goods you mentioned down by the waterfront. Maybe we could do some business, I figured. Instead, I get pounced on!"

Warily the four Bayporters released their captive, who got to his feet. He was about their own age and wore sailors' clothing.

"Sorry if we made a mistake," Frank said. "What's your name?"

"Junior Seetro. I couldn't talk to you earlier because there were too many people around. But I know when sailors act the way you do, they've got hot goods to sell, so I've been following you. Want to discuss it?"

"Sure," Joe replied. "Over here, Junior."

He led the way back to the bench. There was no one else within earshot.

"I saw the guy who was eavesdropping on you before," Junior volunteered. "Looked like a real boy scout. I'd have chased him, too. Now tell me, what've you got?"

"Electronic calculators," Frank replied.

Junior nodded. "I know someone who buys that stuff. He'll pay top dollar. Want to meet him?"

"Why not?" Biff said casually.

"Okay. Hang around while I make a phone call." Junior Seetro went to a phone booth nearby, talked for a few minutes, then returned to the bench.

"It's all set," he announced. "We can go in my car."

He led the way to an old, gray Cadillac in the waterfront parking lot. Frank and Joe looked at each other, both thinking the same thing. Were they walking into a trap? Frank felt it would be worth taking the risk because they outnumbered Junior four to one. He nodded slightly, then the boys put their duffel bags into the trunk and got in the car. Seetro took the wheel and drove about ten miles to a cottage in the woods. It stood in a cove, concealed by trees and thick undergrowth. A boat about fifty feet long was tied to one of the trees.

Junior opened the door and everyone entered except Biff, who felt it was safer for one of them to stay outside. A table in the corner of the front room revealed a collection of valuable objects, including a set of gold candlesticks and two silver pitchers.

Joe nudged his brother. "Maybe that's the stuff stolen from Raymond Wester's house in Bayport!" he whispered.

"But I don't see the missing portrait," Frank whispered back.

Junior had gone to the foot of the stairs and called out, "Mr. N., we're here!" He returned to the group and added, "You've come straight to the top. This man handles most hot cargoes around here."

The same thought flashed through the boys' minds. Would they meet Ignaz Nitron? Biff had heard the conversation through a crack in the door and came in, feeling safe enough to leave his post as guard. He was just in time to see a muscular man with a shock of black hair descending the stairs. Instead of a greeting, he glared at the boys. "You wanted to see me?" he asked gruffly.

"We have a cargo to sell," Frank spoke up. "Junior thought you might be interested."

"Who are you?"

"Sailors. My name's Frank, and these are Joe, Biff, and Chet. We've been working on different merchant ships, mostly out of the West Coast. We picked up this shipment—"

"How do I know I can trust you?" the man grumbled.

Frank decided to take a chance. "You don't," he replied brazenly, "but we heard you were the guy to see."

"Where are the calculators?" he demanded.

"We've got them stashed away on the Florida coast south of Miami," Frank replied quickly. "They're too hot to handle right now. When the heat's off, we'll run them down here in our boat."

Nitron nodded. "Okay. You seem to know what you're doing."

"We've sold our share of hot goods," Chet declared.

"And we haven't been caught yet," Biff maintained.

Nitron rubbed his chin. "I could use you four," he stated. "How about working for me?"

"Okay by me if it's worth our while," Frank replied.

"It will be. The name's Ignaz Nitron. I'll pay you a hundred each for tonight," Nitron went on. "Then you'll get a cut when I complete the deal I have in mind."

"When do we start?" Joe inquired.

"Right now!"

9

A Dangerous Mission

"My men will be over soon," Nitron went on. "We have a cargo to pick up and need extra hands."

As he finished speaking, there was a knock on the door and three men filed into the cottage. They looked at the Bayporters curiously.

"I just hired these guys," Nitron explained and introduced the men. Then he signaled for everyone to leave. The group went to the cove and boarded the boat. Junior Seetro untied the rope, threw it onto the deck, and jumped in after everyone else had gone aboard. Nitron started the engine and soon the smugglers sailed out of the cove.

They followed a course past Key West, Boca Chica Key, and Sugarloaf Key. Just before Big

Pine Key, Nitron turned off the motor. Glancing at his watch, he said, "We'll wait here for the go-ahead."

Some time later a signal came from the shore. A bright light was aimed at a certain point on deck. It blinked on and off at different intervals.

The Hardys realized that someone on Big Pine Key was communicating in Morse code, which they had mastered during their detective training. HONDA COVE NINE O'CLOCK was the message. Then the light went out.

"We don't go in till nine," Nitron stated. "So we gotta kill time. If you want to listen to music, you can use my cassette player below."

The boys went down into the cabin, and a few seconds later Junior Seetro joined them. "I'm glad we got a break," he said, plopping into a chair.

"Why, don't you like to work for Nitron?" Frank asked.

Junior shrugged. "Having to watch out for the law all the time is getting to me. I've never been in prison, but I know a lot of people who have. I'd rather not join them."

"True," Joe spoke up. "But where else can you make this kind of dough?"

"Sometimes I wonder if it's worth it," Junior replied, putting a tape into the player. "Anyway, I have no choice."

"What do you mean?" Chet asked curiously.

Junior sighed. "Aw, nothing. Forget it."

Since the young man did not volunteer any more information, the Hardys decided not to prod him for the time being. Instead, they all began to talk about the group they were listening to.

At eight-thirty Nitron started the motor and headed toward Big Pine Island. Darkness had fallen over the tropical sea, and they could hardly make out where they were going. Nitron entered a shallow cove. Knowing the area like the palm of his hand, he guided the boat expertly to the narrow beach.

Junior jumped onto the sand holding the guide rope, which he tied to a tree. Then everyone went ashore. Nitron signaled with his flashlight.

"Over here!" a muted voice called out.

The smugglers walked toward a secluded spot surrounded by mangroves, where a man stood beside a number of stacked, wooden crates. He came forward and shook hands with Nitron.

"Everything here, Roberto?" Nitron asked.

"Every last crate," Roberto replied. "Now let's finalize the deal. I've got to get back."

Nitron pulled a wad of banknotes out of his pocket and handed them over. Roberto counted them, nodded as if to say the payment was correct, then walked away.

"Let's move the crates onto the boat," Nitron commanded. Two men were required to lift each one, so Frank and Joe took one between them, and lugged it toward the boat.

"I wonder what's in these," Frank whispered. "Feels like bricks!"

Joe nodded. In shifting his grip, he nearly dropped his end of the crate.

"Watch it!" Nitron snarled. "These are expensive Swiss watches, and I don't want any of 'em broken!"

The Hardys lifted their crate onto the boat and went back for another. Chet and Biff did the same. The flurry of activity continued until the last crate was loaded.

During the return voyage, the men were silent. Nitron brought the craft back to the cove on Key Blanco and the boys transferred the crates to the cottage.

Frank and Joe picked up the last one. At that point, they were alone in the boat.

"We'd better blow the whistle on these guys," Joe said. "Those are stolen watches, and we can't let them get away with it."

"If we alert the police now, we'll never find out whether he has Wester's painting," Frank pointed out. "Let's wait awhile and see."

They carried the crate inside and placed it on top of the pile.

Nitron rubbed his hands. "Good job, men," he complimented them. "We'll hold the stuff here for a couple of months. Then we'll sell them when the coast is clear, together with the calculators that are stored south of Miami."

"That gives us time," Frank whispered to Joe.

Nitron handed out everyone's pay, then turned to Frank and Joe. "You two, come on outside. I want to talk to you."

Apprehensively the Hardys followed him to the beach. Was Nitron on to them? If so, their chances of survival were slim since they were outnumbered by the gang!

Nitron suddenly stopped walking and spun around. "I have a dangerous mission coming up," he said. "We'll be sailing for Egret Island off the Dry Tortugas."

"You want us to continue working for you?" Frank inquired cautiously.

Nitron nodded. "But I have to warn you. It's risky. Talk it over with your friends and decide whether you want to come along."

"We're not afraid," Joe spoke up. "Neither are Biff and Chet."

"What's the mission?" Frank inquired.

"Let's just say something very valuable is involved. And the law is all over the place down there. But you'll be paid well."

Nitron would not say any more. He returned to the cottage. Frank and Joe followed and motioned for Chet and Biff to come outside. The four strolled along the beach while Frank described Nitron's offer. "The valuable cargo he mentioned could be the Bolívar portrait," he concluded. "Shall we go along?"

"Of course!" Chet exclaimed. "We've gotten in with these guys, now we have to stick with it until we find what we're looking for."

"Remember, Nitron said it was dangerous."

Chet looked a bit uncomfortable. "Yes. Well, in that case, perhaps one of us should stay here and watch the cottage. I volunteer!"

"No," Biff declared flatly. "We're in the minority and can't afford to lose a single body!"

"All right, all right," Chet gave in. "Let it not be said that Chet Morton left his friends in times of trouble!"

The four returned to the cottage and Frank informed Nitron that they would be going with him. "Let me call a friend who was expecting us," he added.

"Go ahead. Phone's right over there."

Frank dialed Wester's number. "We'll be tied

up working for a while," he said. "Don't worry."

The boys slept in the little building that night while the others stayed on the boat. In the morning, they took off on their voyage westward. Stopping at one of the Tortugas, Nitron allowed his gang to go ashore, but ordered Frank, Joe, Chet, and Biff to stay on board.

"They need a break," he explained. "So I'll let them have a few hours ashore. You keep watch—I'm going to catch some shut-eye."

He went into the cabin. When the boys were sure he was asleep, they began to search the boat for a place where the missing picture might be hidden. However, they found nothing topside.

"It has to be below," Joe stated. "Could be Nitron took it from its frame, rolled it up, and stashed it in one of the lockers."

"Or the safe," Frank added. "You three take the lockers. I'll tackle the safe. But make sure not to wake Nitron or we're finished!"

Stealthily the boys went downstairs. They sneaked past the bunk where Nitron was sleeping, then opened one locker after another. They saw scuba gear, life preservers, nautical charts, and navigation instruments, but there was no sign of the portrait.

Frank, meanwhile, knelt at the safe. He took out the miniature detective kit he carried, removed a small listening device, and placed it next to the dial. Holding his ear against it, he began to turn the knob, trying one combination after another to see if he could find the one that would open the safe.

Suddenly Nitron's voice boomed out behind him. "Hey! What are you doing?"

Frank was paralyzed for a moment, and his mouth went dry. Slowly he turned around, desperately hoping to find a way out of his predicament.

He gaped in surprise. Nitron was not standing behind him as he had expected. The smuggler was still lying on his bunk with his eyes closed! His lips moved. "What're you doing?" he repeated. "You taking this stuff to Key Largo? If so, I want my cut. I'll tell—" The rest of the sentence came out in an unintelligible mumble.

Frank breathed a sigh of relief. He's talking in his sleep! he thought. Boy, that was a close call!

Still shaking slightly, he turned back to the safe, trying several more combinations. At last the tumblers fell into place. Silently, a fraction of an inch at a time, he pulled the door open and looked in.

The safe was empty!

10

The Alchemist

Frank quietly closed the safe, sneaked past the sleeping Nitron, and made his way up to the deck. The others were already there.

"Nothing in the safe," he reported.

"Nothing at all?" Chet asked incredulously.

"No. I can't—" He stopped short when he heard footsteps. Nitron came up from the cabin carrying a nautical chart, which he spread out on a locker at the stern of the boat.

"Here's Egret Island," he told the boys, indicating the spot with his finger. "It's roughly halfway between Florida and the Dry Tortugas. Our problem is the police that patrol the waters around there."

"They might stop us," Joe noted.

Nitron nodded. "That's why I said this was a dangerous mission. If the cops cut us off, I want you and Junior to go into action. Start a fight and distract them, so I can take off with the goods and the other three men."

"And leave us to be the fall guys?" Joe asked, not believing his ears.

"I'll pay you five hundred apiece for this. If you're caught, it's up to you to work your way out."

The boys stared at each other. "Now I get it!" Frank said through clenched teeth. "You hired us so your regular crew doesn't have to stick their necks out!"

Nitron shrugged. "Five hundred. Take it or leave it."

Just then Nitron's crew straggled in from their shore leave. Nitron explained his strategy to them, then started the engine and guided the boat toward Egret Island.

The Bayport youths conversed in low tones. "We can't help these creeps against the police!" Biff declared.

"We won't," Frank replied. "But we'll have to stay around as long as we can to find the painting!"

Junior ambled up to them. "It figures," he

grumbled. "Who gets the dangerous end of the stick? Not him and his old buddies, oh no! *We* have to protect them so they can take the booty and run!"

"Has he pulled this before?" Biff asked.

"Sure. It's always me or someone like me."

"Then why do you hang around?"

"If I don't, I won't be around, period. You think I wanted to get you guys into this? He forced me, because he's got the goods on me. Now you're in the same boat."

"I don't understand," Biff spoke up. "He can't turn you in to the police!"

"Who's talking about the police? He's got his own henchmen to do the job. And they don't put you in the slammer, either. They put you on the bottom of the sea!" Junior shrugged helplessly. "You guys are all right. I really like you. Sorry for getting you into this, but I had no choice."

"I'm glad you told us," Frank said cautiously. "Perhaps we can find a way out. Let's think about it for a while."

Just then Nitron stopped the boat. Egret Island came into view on the horizon. He picked up a pair of high-powered binoculars and carefully scanned the shore.

"There's a launch," he reported. "It's going from

north to south. We'll move in right after it's left, and just hope the next one doesn't appear too quickly."

His face tense, Nitron ran the boat close to the island and turned north. The boys noticed vacation homes facing the water. Farther on, there were only trees and thickets. Flocks of white birds with long sinuous necks flew overhead. "Those are egrets," Frank observed.

Nitron headed for shore, past a tangle of tall trees, vines, and thick mangrove roots. Soon they were gliding through a deep cove that extended inland for a hundred yards. At the end, Junior Seetro jumped onto the beach with the rope and tied up the boat.

Nitron called everyone on deck. "Boys," he said, "you stay here and guard the boat. The rest come with me."

"And when the cops show, we do 'em in single-handedly," Junior grumbled as the smugglers went ashore. Then he turned to Frank. "Have you come up with any ideas?"

"I'm working on it. Tell me, what do you know about this mission to Egret Island?"

"Nothing. I've been here with them before, but they always left me to watch the boat. I never saw what the others did."

"Would you be willing to go to the police and blow the whistle on these guys?" Joe asked.

"You kiddin'? I've no proof. The cops wouldn't believe me. The best they'd do is let me go and start snooping around, and then Nitron would know I squealed and do me in."

"They'd believe *us*!" Frank declared.

"Oh, sure. Who are you but just another bunch of kids on the shady side of the law!"

"We're detectives," Frank said. "The police know we're working underground. We're Frank and Joe Hardy."

"Hardy?" Junior's eyes grew round as saucers. "You mean, *the* Hardy boys?"

"Yes. We came here to find a priceless painting that Nitron stole from a man in Bayport. It's a portrait of Simón Bolívar. Have you seen it?"

Junior shook his head. "No, I haven't. Man, are you really the Hardy boys?"

"Believe it," Chet said. "They're working on a case, and Biff and I are helping them."

"Look, we haven't much time to waste," Joe spoke up. "Do you know where Nitron goes when he comes to Egret Island, Junior?"

"I once heard him mention a hill at the head of the cove, past a tall palm tree, and beyond a pond."

"All right," Frank said. "Joe and I'll go and see

whether we can find out anything. If the smugglers come back, just tell them we went into the woods for some coconuts, okay?"

"Okay!" Junior declared. "And if you can get us all out of this racket and save our skins, I'll never do anything illegal again!"

Joe grinned. "We'll take you up on that!"

Moments later the Hardys were pushing through the undergrowth at the head of the cove. They followed a trail of broken branches and footprints in the sandy ground where the smugglers obviously had passed. The path slanted upward. Soon the boys found themselves at the top of the hill.

"There's the palm tree," Joe declared, pointing. "But I don't see a pond."

"Only one thing to do," Frank decided. He took off his jacket and shoes, got a grip on the tree with his hands and feet, then worked his way up until he could grab the fronds and survey the area.

"There it is," he called out. "And a barn's on the other side. That might be the place we're looking for."

He slid down the tree and put his shoes and jacket on again. The boys went to the pond, circled around it, and stopped at a clump of scrubby trees. Through the branches they could see a long wooden barn one story high with a loft above. Dense black smoke poured from the chimney.

"Somebody's home," Frank muttered.

They slipped stealthily through the bushes until they stood at the side of an open window. Cautiously they peered in.

The first thing they saw was a blazing furnace in the middle of the room. Steam poured out of its vents. Molten metal dripped into a cast-iron ramp and from there into a cast-iron vat.

A barrel filled with lumps of lead stood on one side of the furnace, a container holding slag on the other. Ladles, scoops, and tongs lay on the floor. On the wall hung a table of astrological signs, and nearby an illustration of the planets circling the sun. Across the sun the word GOLD was written in large letters.

"I don't believe this!" Joe whispered. "It looks like the lab of a mad scientist!"

An old man was standing near a table holding a test tube containing a golden liquid from which wisps of white vapor drifted upward. With his other hand he tugged his long white beard. He wore a golden robe dotted with black stars, and a tall hat in the shape of a cone.

"Gold, show thyself!" he intoned as he gazed at the test tube.

"He's an alchemist," Frank muttered.

The old man set the test tube in a rack and walked to the furnace. He picked up a small ladle and, muttering to himself, looked at the molten metal dripping into the vat. Then he pushed the ladle into a pocket of his robe.

A younger man wearing ordinary clothing came in from the back room. "Professor Viga, Nitron and his men are waiting in the woods outside."

"Tell them to come into the back room, Myer. We can talk there," the alchemist replied. Then both men left the lab and closed the door behind them. Silence fell, except for the sputtering of the furnace.

"If we go inside," Joe suggested, "we might be able to eavesdrop."

Frank nodded. "Let's climb through the window." Grasping the frame with both hands and kicking off with his feet, he vaulted up. Then he swung his legs through the window and let himself down gently. Joe followed.

The Hardys moved quickly toward the other side of the lab, stepping over odd gadgets and geometrical forms made of wood, metal, and stone.

"These are supposed to give you voodoo powers," Joe whispered, pointing to a number of spheres and pyramids.

"Mumbo jumbo." Frank chuckled.

In the middle of the room, they felt the intense heat from the furnace and from the liquid metal dripping down the ramp into the vat. Suddenly Frank skidded on a stone sphere the size of a marble. He lost his balance and plunged toward the vat of molten lead!

11

The Heirloom

Joe clutched wildly at his brother. His fingers caught Frank's jacket and he yanked him back in the nick of time.

"Are you okay?" Joe asked anxiously.

"Fine," Frank assured him. "As long as I don't have to take a bath in that tub! Thanks, Joe."

Shuddering after his close call, Frank turned away from the furnace and moved toward the door. Joe was right behind him. The Hardys could hear the murmur of voices, but not what was being said. Frank gently lifted the latch and pushed the door open a crack. All they could see was a barrel of slag, or burned-out lead, but now they could hear everything!

"Professor Viga, have you turned lead into gold yet?" Nitron demanded.

"Not yet," Viga admitted. "But I think I know the formula. A few more experiments, and I will have made the discovery of the century!"

"He's a nut," Joe whispered.

Nitron walked to the slag barrel where the Hardys could see him. Myer also came into view next to him.

Pointing to the barrel, the smuggler asked, "Is this the burned-out lead?"

"Yes," Viga replied.

Surreptitiously, Nitron slipped a lump of yellow metal from his pocket and held it behind his back. Myer took it and secretly dropped it into the container, all the while continuing the conversation with the eccentric old man.

"He 'salted' the slag," Frank whispered, referring to the trick used by crooks of planting something in a certain place, then pretending to find it.

Suddenly Myer shouted, "Gold!" He reached into the barrel and pulled out the yellow lump that he had tossed in. He held it up for Viga to see. It gave off a soft gleam.

Viga hurried over and seized it. "I must have overlooked this piece!" he croaked. "Is there any more? Let me see!" Excitedly he foraged in the barrel, tossing pieces of burned-out lead over his shoulder. His head disappeared bit by bit.

At last he stood up again. "There's no more," he said, disappointed. Then he brightened up. "But this lump proves my formula's correct. All I have to do is review my experiments and find out which one will produce gold every time. Then you can sell it on the world market, Mr. Nitron, and we'll be millionaires!"

Nitron nodded. "But right now we have a little problem," he pointed out. "You said you'd make enough gold to finance the business. I've run out of funds completely, so you'd better give me that family heirloom you mentioned to tide us over until you make your gold."

Viga nodded. "I'll stick to our bargain. Soon we'll have all the gold we need, and I'll buy the heirloom back."

Nitron shrugged. "Fine. I'll borrow money on it to pay the bills until you start mass-producing."

Viga reached inside his robe and pulled out a black jewel case. Opening it, he displayed a beautiful diamond necklace.

Frank nudged Joe. "That's the valuable object Nitron was talking about, not the Wester picture!"

Nitron took the necklace and held it up. The stones glittered brilliantly.

"It belonged to my mother," Viga said. "That's why I don't want to part with it forever."

"I'll take good care of it," Nitron assured him with a cynical grin. He put the necklace into the case again, slipped it into his pants pocket, and grabbed Viga's hand. "And now we'll have to get back to Key Blanco."

There was a shuffling of boots on the floor as the smugglers got to their feet. Frank and Joe quickly retreated across the laboratory, when suddenly the furnace erupted with a roar! Flames shot up and the vents spewed clouds of steam. Molten lead streamed down into the vat, while the safety valve went off with a shrill scream!

The force shook the floor of the building. The next instant the door to the back room burst wide open. The Hardys were revealed in the glare of the blazing furnace!

"Frank and Joe, what are you doing here?" Nitron demanded. "I ordered you to stay on the boat!"

The boys turned and ran across the lab.

"They're spies!" Nitron screamed. "Catch 'em!"

He and his smugglers rushed up to the young detectives who had no chance to climb through the window. They circled around to the other side of the furnace, where a tall ladder led to the loft.

Joe spotted a large box full of marble-sized stone

spheres marked with the mystical stars of alchemy. He scooped up a handful and hurled them under the feet of their pursuers. Nitron and his men began to slip and slide. They lost their balance and grabbed wildly at one another. Then they fell in a heap on the floor.

The Hardys scrambled up the ladder to the loft. Frantically they looked around for a window or skylight that would let them out onto the roof. But there was no exit of any kind! Joe tried to kick the ladder down. Too late! The smugglers were already swarming up toward the loft.

"We're trapped!" Joe exclaimed.

Frank pulled his brother into a niche in the wall next to the ladder, gesturing for him to be silent.

One by one, Myer and the smugglers climbed from the ladder into the loft and, not seeing the Hardys, rushed to the other side. Nitron came last. As he stepped into the loft, Viga's jewel case, which was protruding from his back pocket, fell out. Not noticing it, the smuggler rushed to the rear, where his companions were shouting and looking for the boys.

Frank quickly grabbed the jewel case, then he and Joe skidded down the ladder, pulling it after them to the floor. Nitron and his men heard the noise and gathered at the edge of the loft. They yelled furiously and shook their fists.

Viga had watched the chase in dazed silence. Now he spoke up. "What is this all about?"

"They're smugglers!" Frank hissed as the boys turned to run out of the building. "Criminals. Here's your necklace. Don't give it back to them!" He shoved the jewel case at the bewildered old man. Then he rushed outside with Joe at his heels.

Viga followed. "Wait!" he called out. "You mean all my alchemy was for nothing?"

"That's right, Professor," Frank said, grabbing the man's arm. "Come on. You should report this to the police. That lump of gold was planted by Myer. We saw the whole thing. He only pretended to find it in the barrel."

Viga was aghast. "My assistant? He's one of them?"

"He is," Frank confirmed, dragging the professor along as they moved rapidly back toward the boat. Unfortunately, Viga held them up. The alchemist's ladle in his pocket weighed him down, and he had to hold his robe above his ankles with one hand to avoid tripping on it. His cone-shaped hat kept slipping down over his eyes, forcing him to push it back in order to see where he was going.

By the time the group reached the top of the hill, Viga was panting and puffing.

"Please keep going, Professor," Joe encouraged him. "We're almost there."

"The smugglers must have climbed down from the loft by now," Frank said. "I'm sure they're hot on our trail."

Sounds in the underbrush behind them indicated that Nitron and his gang were drawing near. Desperately the Hardys hurried the old man down the hill. Finally they saw the boat, with Chet, Biff, and Junior Seetro on deck waving at them.

Just then Viga tripped over his gown and fell. His hat tumbled off, and the boys had to stop and help him to his feet.

Nitron and his men leaped out of the underbrush and attacked them! Chet, Biff, and Junior jumped ashore and plunged into the fight. A wild melee ensued. Biff landed a roundhouse right that leveled one of the smugglers. Chet, swinging his arms with hands clasped, pounded another in the stomach and made him double over.

Frank wrestled with Nitron, and Joe got a hammerlock on Myer. Viga stood stock-still at first, then he took his alchemist's ladle out of his pocket and struck Nitron on the head with a loud *bong*. The smuggler blacked out. Then the old man did the same to Myer. He went down the line swinging his weapon till every one of the gang lay on the ground unconscious!

Grinning, the boys got to their feet. "Nice work, Professor," Frank said. "You deserve a medal!"

"We'd better get those guys tied up before they come to," Joe advised.

"No trouble," Junior replied. He ran to the boat and returned with a coil of rope and a sailor's knife. Cutting the rope into sections, he handed them around, and the boys tied the hands of the smugglers behind their backs.

Nitron awoke first. The Hardys made him go aboard and sit down on deck. The rest of the gang followed. "We'll take them straight to police headquarters," Frank said.

He started the engine and steered the boat out into open water. Halfway down the coast a police launch appeared and cut across their bow. An officer with a bullhorn ordered Frank to heave to. Nodding, the boy let the vessel come to a stop.

The police launch eased up alongside, and a lieutenant came aboard. Surveying the men on deck, he demanded, "What's going on here?"

"That's Ignaz Nitron and his gang of smugglers," Frank said. "We caught them as they were about to defraud Professor Viga."

"What!" The lieutenant stared in surprise as Frank explained the details of their mission.

"You've done an excellent job," he said at the end. "We've been trying to catch these guys for a long time. Now, thanks to you, we've got them!"

12

Everglades Adventure

The lieutenant turned to Viga. "Want to tell us about your part in all this, Professor?"

"I believe in alchemy," Viga confessed. "I needed a laboratory, and Myer helped me establish one in the barn. Later he brought Nitron to see me. They pretended to believe I could turn lead into gold. I know now I was deceived."

"Lieutenant, it was a confidence game," Frank said. "Nitron and Myer salted the slag with a lump of gold and then claimed to find it."

"They were after the professor's diamond necklace all the time," Joe commented. "They tricked him into giving it to them. He would have never gotten it back if Frank hadn't disrupted their scheme."

Viga sighed. "I read every book on alchemy, and carried out many experiments, always hoping my furnace would produce gold. And all for nothing!" He buried his head in his hands and groaned in despair.

"The furnace is still going in the lab," Joe pointed out.

"I'll have one of my men shut it down," the lieutenant said and dispatched an officer to the barn. Then, after advising them of their legal rights, he interrogated the gang. Confronted with the evidence, Nitron confessed he had tricked Viga into giving him the necklace.

"What about Raymond Wester's picture?" Frank demanded.

Nitron looked startled. "What do you know about that?" he exploded.

"We found your fingerprint in his house in Bayport. You and Mark Morphy took the picture."

"With the help of Tom," Joe added. "You also stole two golden candlesticks and silver pitchers, which you hid in your cottage on Key Blanco along with other things you lifted—"

Nitron, who had turned white as a sheet, interrupted nervously. "We took the picture, I admit.

But in Blanco City Morphy went off with it. I have no idea where it is!"

Nitron's men assured the lieutenant that they did not know either, and were led away into the police launch for transport to Egret Island.

The boys followed, steering Nitron's boat, and gave a full report of what had happened.

"We now have enough evidence to put this gang behind bars for a long time," the lieutenant said. "Thanks for your excellent work, boys."

"What about Junior Seetro?" Frank asked.

"Well, he has been an accomplice, and we'll have to see what the authorities say. In the meantime we'll have to ask him not to leave the area. He has to be available for the trial as a witness."

"*That*, I'm glad of," Junior promised. "I'm really happy to be out of this racket—I'll tell everything I know!"

The lieutenant turned to the Hardys. "When you get to Blanco City, it would be a great help if you led the local police to Nitron's cottage."

"We'll be glad to," Frank replied.

"Good. I'll notify them that you're coming."

The boys rented a boat for the return voyage. On the way, they discussed the smugglers.

Suddenly Frank had an idea. "Junior, was anyone else involved in Nitron's operation?"

"Not directly," their new friend replied. "But now that you mention it, he did say he got certain orders from the chief in written messages left in a place in the Everglades."

"Where?" Biff asked.

"Can't tell you, fellows. All I know is that it's near Moss Tributary."

"I remember that from the map," Frank noted. "It's west of the Pa-hay-okee Trail."

Reaching Blanco City, the boys turned in the boat, then reported to the police. Together with two officers, they sped to Nitron's cottage and helped load the crates of Swiss watches and other stolen objects onto the truck they had brought. When they were finished, one of the policemen said, "We'll return all these goods to their rightful owners once we have established who they are."

He thanked the young detectives, then the officers drove off while the boys returned to Blanco City in Junior Seetro's car. There the Hardys and their friends shook hands with Junior. "Good luck," Joe said, while Frank took their duffel bags out of the trunk. "And remember your promise!"

Junior grinned. "Let's hope that next time you see me, I'll be in the Merchant Marine, straight as an arrow!"

He drove off and the other four walked along the

cliff to Smugglers Cove. When they entered Wester's house, the maid failed to recognize them until they spoke to her.

"I thought you were sailors," she confessed.

"It's just a disguise," Joe told her. "Is Mr. Wester in?"

"No. He's gone to Key West for several days, but he wants you to stay here until he gets back. Come on in."

The boys went up to their rooms and changed into their regular clothes. They put their sailors' outfits and beards into the duffel bags, which they gave to the maid to donate to a charitable organization.

"Hey, how about some flapjacks?" Chet proposed. "I'm starved."

"So am I," the others said in unison.

"Come on downstairs. The makings are in the refrigerator. I saw them the other night when I went for my snack."

In the kitchen, Chet got the cook's permission to use the stove. Pouring batter into a frying pan, he hummed merrily, then tossed half-fried flapjacks into the air, flipping them over expertly, and caught them in the pan again. Soon he had a sizable pile of pancakes on a platter beside the stove.

The other three set the kitchen table and poured

milk. Chet set the platter down in the middle of the table. "Chef's specialty," he boasted with a grin.

The boys attacked the treat with great appetite. When they were finished, they cleaned up the kitchen and went to Frank's room to size up the situation.

"Well, this was an interesting experience," Biff started. "But we haven't found the picture."

"Junior mentioned that some chief gave orders to Nitron," Frank said. "And Fatso talked about a chief on the plane. Maybe it's the same guy."

"He left the messages for Nitron in the Everglades," Joe added. "That should be our next stop!"

It was decided that Frank and Joe would look for the chief, while Chet and Biff would stay in Harrison Wester's house—to wait for Wester's return and to watch for Morphy. Then, exhausted after the excitement of their trip and the capture of the smugglers, the boys went to bed and slept soundly until morning.

After breakfast the Hardys were ready to leave.

"We'll tell Mr. Wester what's happened if he gets back before you do," Biff promised.

"Just say hello to the alligators for me," Chet quipped. "Sorry I can't go swimming with them."

"We'd better get moving," Frank said with a

grin. "Our best bet is to take the ferry to Flamingo on the southern tip of the mainland. From there we'll make our way into the Everglades."

The young detectives walked into Blanco City and were soon aboard the ferry on the Gulf of Mexico. When they arrived, they went to the Flamingo Visitors' Center, past the lines of small boats tied to the docks. Frank bought a map at the information desk, while Joe studied an announcement on a bulletin board nearby. It stated that alligators were an endangered species and that hunting them without a license was illegal.

"How do we get to Moss Tributary?" Frank asked the woman behind the counter.

She consulted her detailed guidebook. "Take the bus up the Mangrove Trail to the Pa-hay-okee Trail. There you can rent a boat and follow the map west."

"Thanks."

Frank and Joe went to the terminal and boarded the bus. Luckily they did not have to wait long for its departure. On the Mangrove Trail they saw trees with great bunches of roots that arched through the air and then grew down into the swampy earth below. Soon they came to an area of grass and trees not too different from what they had seen farther north.

"Hey, Frank, this isn't bad," Joe exclaimed.

"Maybe we won't drown in the swamp after all!"

"Forget it," Frank replied. "Moss Tributary is in the real Everglades. We'll get our feet wet for sure."

At the Pa-hay-okee Trail, the Hardys rented a flat-bottomed skiff along with leather boots for walking. Joe took the controls, while Frank checked the map as they chugged west.

They found themselves moving through a wilderness of water, mud, and mangrove trees broken up by higher and dryer areas. In certain places it was possible to walk for hundreds of yards on dry land. But the rest was a morass of shallow winding streams, often joining one another only to separate farther downstream. Acres of grass pushed out of the mud to a height of six feet or more.

Egrets and other birds rose in flocks as the boys passed. Fish broke the surface of the water, and snakes slithered over the ground. Alligators cruised along the streams with their snouts barely visible, seeking their prey.

"This looks like the end of the world to me!" Joe complained. "How are we ever going to find a clue in this desolate swamp?"

For the first time since they began their search, Frank shared his brother's doubts. Hopelessly he looked around him. "I really don't know!" he said.

13

The Rattlesnake

The Hardys kept moving for several miles. The sound of their motor mingled with the cries of birds, the scream of bobcats, and the rustle of mangroves in the wind.

"Boy, we really are a long way from nowhere," Frank complained.

A broader expanse of water caught Joe's eye. "Looks like a lake up ahead," he announced. "We're heading right into it."

Frank plotted the area on his map. "It's called Moss Pond. Five streams run together here, which makes it the biggest lake in this part of the Everglades."

They chugged into the shallow expanse of water bordered by marsh grass.

"The Moss River is number four," Frank said.

Joe twisted the steering wheel and guided the skiff into the direction his brother had indicated. "How far to Moss Tributary?" he asked.

"A few miles," Frank replied. "It's the only stream that runs into this river."

When they reached Moss Tributary and turned toward it, Joe said, "Now that we're here, we don't even know what to look for."

"It has to be a building, don't you think? But keep an eye peeled for anything. No telling what we'll run into."

They entered a desolate area with swamps on one side and dry, rough terrain covered with tangled vegetation on the other. Mangroves were spread out everywhere.

Suddenly Joe spotted a wisp of black smoke curling into the sky. Quickly he shut off the engine and let the skiff drift to a stop.

"What's up?" Frank asked.

Joe pointed to the smoke. "Somebody got here before us."

"Let's check it out," Frank said, excited.

The boys picked up a couple of paddles, quietly dipped them into the water, and moved the boat over to a clump of tall grass. Parting it, they saw the remains of a campfire. The wood was still smoking.

"Nobody here," Joe stated. "Let's see if we can find a clue."

"But be careful!" Frank warned.

Paddling to the site, they climbed out of their skiff and explored the area. Footprints were grouped around the fire.

"I count four different people," Frank announced after examining the prints closely. "I wonder where they went."

"Well, the fire's still smoking, so they were here only a few minutes ago," Joe deduced. "If they'd gone downstream, we'd have met them. Therefore, they must have gone upstream."

Frank nodded. "I hope we can pick up their trail. But we'd better watch out. If they hear us, they might set a trap for us!"

"Right. Let's paddle up as quietly as we can," Joe agreed.

After stamping out the smoldering embers, they went back to their skiff and continued along Moss Tributary. Half an hour later, they heard the sound of voices ahead.

"I wonder if they're park rangers," Joe said.

Frank shook his head. "Not a chance. Rangers wouldn't leave smoking embers. Too much danger of starting a fire."

The Hardys turned into the mouth of a small stream feeding Moss Tributary, then tied their skiff to a mangrove root. Under the cover of the trees, they followed the sound of the voices until they spotted a boat at the bank.

Four men were inside, all carrying high-power rifles.

"I don't recognize any of them," Frank whispered. "Do you?"

"Never saw them before," Joe replied. "I wonder what they're up to."

"We'll have to get closer to find out."

Silently the boys slipped through the mangroves until they found a hiding place among the giant roots of a tree. They had a clear view of the men in the boat, whose conversation was now clearly audible.

One of them patted his rifle and boasted, "We'll get plenty of 'gators this time."

"Long as the park rangers don't butt in!" said another.

"We'll take care of them if they do!" a third spoke up. "We've got enough ammo to fight a war!" He rapped his knuckles on a box labeled **Ammunition.**

The men laughed loudly, and began to joke about shooting alligators.

"Who cares if it's illegal as long as we make big

money?" one asked. "There's such a market overseas for skins—belts, handbags, wallets, watchbands, you know . . ."

Joe recalled the sign at the Flamingo Visitors' Center warning that the Everglades alligator was an endangered species that ought to be protected. He nudged Frank and whispered, "Poachers! We can't let them get away with it! But there're too many of them for us to tackle. What'll we do?"

"Lie low," Frank advised. "That's all we *can* do right now."

Suddenly footsteps approached from the upstream area. The men jumped out of their boat and crouched next to it.

"Might be the rangers!" one of them rasped. "Let's give 'em a friendly reception!"

All four raised their rifles and pointed them in the direction of the footsteps. Then the bushes parted and two men appeared, both carrying rifles. One was tall and muscular, the other shorter and heavy.

"Tom and Fatso!" Joe hissed.

Dumbfounded, the Hardys watched the pair walk up to the boat, where the men lowered their guns and greeted the newcomers with friendly grins.

"We'll have a clear shot at the 'gators," the tall man said, "or my name isn't Tom Lami."

"How about the park rangers?" one of the men wanted to know.

"They'll never catch us," Fatso retorted. "We saw 'em patrol the alligator pool, then they moved on. Never knew we were watching 'em!"

"Biggest concentration of 'gators I ever saw," Tom continued. "We'll start hunting tomorrow."

"It's like shootin' fish in a barrel." Fatso smirked.

Suddenly a terrific clatter broke out overhead, a deafening sound that echoed across the Everglades. The poachers ducked for cover under mangroves some distance from the Hardys.

A helicopter zoomed through the sky toward the area. The emblem, EVERGLADES PARK RANGERS, was painted on its side.

"If we could only signal the pilot!" Joe muttered. "Then he could send a patrol here and nab these guys!"

"Maybe he'll spot their boat," Frank said. "I doubt he'll see ours. We hid it too well."

Tensely the young detectives watched the chopper coming closer and circling overhead. The pilot looked down at Moss Tributary, and said something to his copilot. Then the craft moved off, but returned a few moments later.

"Would he be coming back for a second look if he hadn't seen the boat?" Frank whispered.

"Maybe he's calling headquarters on his radio," Joe guessed.

But they observed the pilot shaking his head. The chopper completed another circle and flew off, the sound of its propellers diminishing in the distance.

"He didn't see the boat," Frank said, disappointed. "It must be too far under the trees."

"That leaves us to deal with the poachers!" Joe said.

"Six against two isn't very good odds. We need a miracle to help us in this situation."

"I still think we should forget the chief for a while until we save the alligators," Joe concluded.

The poachers came out of their hiding place, grinning triumphantly.

"Those rangers didn't see us," Fatso exclaimed. "We're safe."

"Right," Tom Lami agreed. "Now let's get this show on the road. No sense in wasting any more time." The men walked over to their boat and Tom untied the rope.

Frank and Joe stood up, looking after them. Just then the older Hardy boy felt a slithering movement over his boot. He looked down and froze with fright. A rattlesnake stared at him with open jaws and extended fangs, ready to strike!

14

The Poachers' Camp

Frank stood stock-still for an instant, then kicked his foot violently—just in time to prevent the snake's sharp fangs from reaching him. The rattler flew through the air and landed with a thump on the bank near the boat.

The noise caused the poachers to whirl around.

"The rangers!" Fatso hissed. "Knock 'em off!"

Six rifles pointed in the direction of the rattlesnake as it slithered out of the underbrush. Frightened by the men the reptile vanished among the roots of a tree.

"It's only a snake," Lami said, lowering his gun. "Let's get going. We'll establish a base camp at the big bend upstream. It's near the alligator pool."

The boat moved away from the bank and chugged up Moss Tributary. The Hardys, still shaken from their close call, came out from under the mangroves and watched it till the poachers were out of sight.

"Lucky they didn't see us!" Joe muttered.

Frank nodded. "We'll have to go after them. Too bad we don't have backups. I wish Chet and Biff were here."

"Let's radio the rangers," Joe suggested. "Maybe they can get here in time to give us some help."

Returning to their skiff, he used its radio to contact the headquarters of the park rangers. A sergeant answered.

"Alligator poachers on Moss Tributary," Joe reported tensely. "Send help fast."

"Patrol boat will be on the way," the sergeant promised after hearing the details.

When Joe hung up, Frank pointed to a spot on the map. "Here's where Moss Tributary cuts to the west and then back to the east. That must be the bend Lami talked about. We can catch up with them there."

"Right."

The Hardys pushed off with Joe again at the controls. After traveling for about five miles, Frank signaled to his brother to cut the engine.

"The big bend's beginning right here," he said in an undertone. "We'll have to paddle now."

They worked their way upstream until they spotted the poachers' boat tied up at the bank. Quietly they fastened their own craft under mangrove branches hanging low over the water, then sneaked through the underbrush. They were guided by the sound of voices to a spot where another large cluster of roots offered them cover.

They saw the poachers sitting around a campfire cooking hamburgers on a grill. The aroma made Joe's nose twitch. "Too bad we can't barge in and say we're backpackers," he whispered. "Maybe they'd treat us to a couple of burgers!"

"I'd have mine with ketchup," Frank continued the joke. Then he was serious again. "We'll have to settle for fruit," he added. "Come on."

Silently the Hardys retreated farther into the trees. When they were sure the poachers could not hear them, they plucked pieces of fruit from the mangroves and made a meal of them.

By the time the boys crawled back to their hiding place near the camp, night had fallen. The fire threw weird shadows over the area and tongues of flame reflected on the surface of Moss Tributary.

The poachers had finished their meal and began polishing their rifles.

"After shootin' the 'gators," Tom said, "we'll bring the skins here and pile 'em in the boat. I reckon it'll hold at least a couple dozen."

"Good idea," Fatso agreed. "And that box of ammo will keep us in bullets as long as we need to hunt."

Frank nudged Joe with his elbow. "We can foul up their plans if we grab the ammo box," he whispered.

Joe replied in the same undertone, "When they go to sleep, maybe we'll get a chance."

Just then Fatso stood up. "I'll find some more wood," he announced and walked directly toward the mangrove where the Hardys were hiding! Both boys hunched down between the roots. Their hearts pounded as they wondered what to do if they were discovered.

However, at the last moment the man turned in a different direction. He had spotted a number of dead branches lying under another tree. Gathering an armful, he returned to the camp and dropped the wood on the fire. It blazed in the darkness of the night.

"I wonder where the Hardys are," Tom Lami said suddenly.

Startled, Frank and Joe strained their ears to hear the answer.

Fatso threw a stick in the fire. "We ain't seen

'em since that time in the Bayport Hotel. They musta got scared off the case."

Lami sounded dubious. "Then who were those two kids who jumped me in the alley in Homestead? It was too dark for me to see 'em, but they could've been Frank and Joe Hardy."

"Maybe. But wouldn't we have spotted 'em on the plane?" Fatso argued. "Those other two kids who tailed us seemed to be out for some kicks. I thought they were just talking through their hats when they mentioned poachers."

"I'd still feel better if you'd have run 'em down," Lami said venomously.

"So would I," Fatso agreed. "But they got out of the way too fast."

"Where are Nitron and Morphy?" one of the men asked.

"Nitron's still working out of Key Blanco," Tom replied. "As for Morphy, I have no idea where he is. He took off with the picture when he was supposed to see the chief."

"I'd like to know who this chief guy is," Fatso put in.

Tom shrugged. "Nobody knows. He leaves written messages at the stone house near here. That's how me and Nitron get our orders. But we never met him."

Frank and Joe listened with bated breath. Apparently both the smugglers and the poachers had the same boss. But the poachers had no idea that Nitron and his people were in jail on Egret Island! Now the next step for the young detectives was to find the stone house Tom had mentioned.

"Let's hit the sack," one of the men said. "We have a big day tomorrow."

"Good idea," said another. "I'm beat."

The gang lay down on the ground and prepared to go to sleep around the smoldering fire. Lami assigned three of them to spell one another on guard duty. The man responsible for the first watch sat with his back against a tree, holding his rifle across his knees. Soon all was quiet.

The Hardys discussed in whispers what to do.

"Let's untie their boat and make it drift downstream," Joe suggested.

Frank shook his head. "It might get stuck in the mud where the gang can recover it. We'd better drop the ammo box overboard. But we can't as long as the guy with the gun is around."

Rustling in a mangrove tree caused the guard to get to his feet and walk over for a look. Suddenly an unearthly scream in the branches startled him so much that he dropped his rifle.

A bobcat leaped to the ground, screamed again, then ran off. Muttering angrily to himself, the guard picked up his weapon and resumed his post.

He yawned, then began to nod. Finally he fell asleep.

The Hardys heard him snore. Otherwise, there was no sound anywhere in the camp.

"Now's our chance," Frank whispered.

Quickly he and Joe clambered out from among the mangrove roots. They felt raindrops coming down through the leaves, and distant thunder broke the stillness.

"Hurry up before we get drenched," Frank muttered as they crept through the undergrowth and circled the camp on their way to the water's edge.

They passed within a few yards of the guard, then stepped into the boat. Cautiously they moved to the stern where the ammunition box was. Each boy took one end of the heavy crate and eased it over the gunwale. Slowly they lowered the box into the water and grinned as it sank to the bottom.

15

The Storm

Suddenly a lightning bolt flashed across the sky, lighting up the campsite. In the glare, the Hardys saw that the mud in the bed of Moss Tributary had all but covered the ammunition box.

"It's gone for good!" Frank said triumphantly. "Come on, let's get out of here."

Stooping low to avoid detection in case the lightning had awakened the poachers, the young detectives scrambled out of the boat.

"I spotted an alligator den earlier," Joe revealed. "It's almost like a cave. We can go in there for shelter."

"Suppose there are 'gators in it?" Frank asked.

"Let's hope there aren't. They might have left

after the gang got here," Joe said. He led the way to a point in the bank where the giant lizards had made a small cave by gouging out the soft earth. Frank pulled his pencil flashlight from his pocket, leaned over the edge, and directed its beam into the cave. It was empty, and showed no signs that alligators had been there recently.

Relieved, the Hardys crawled into the den, which was just big enough for the two of them. Protected from the storm, they watched the rain turn into a downpour. High winds began to lash the mangroves, while thunder and lightning hurtled across the night sky.

Suddenly they heard footsteps and angry shouting overhead as the poachers took refuge under the mangrove trees.

"They're near enough to touch," Frank murmured. "I hope they don't find us."

"So do I," Joe agreed fervently.

The storm died away just as dawn was breaking. After hearing the poachers move away, the Hardys crawled out of the alligator den and sneaked up to the gang's camp. They saw that the boat had disappeared.

"The storm yanked it loose from the tree!" Tom yelled to his men. "Go find it!"

Fatso shielded his eyes with his hand and peered downstream. "It's stuck in the mud!" he exclaimed. "About a hundred yards from here near the bank." He ordered two of the men to bring the boat back. They maneuvered it into its old position and tied it to the tree again.

Tom Lami stared in consternation. "Where's the ammo box?"

The gang gathered at the water's edge and looked in dismay at the empty corner where the box had been. Fatso offered a suggestion. "The storm musta knocked it overboard. If we find it, we can salvage the bullets. The box is waterproof."

He ordered an immediate search of the stream from the camp down to the point where the boat had been found. But one by one the poachers returned to say that they had failed to discover any sign of the box.

"Musta sunk in the mud," Fatso guessed. "We'll never find it. What do we do now—give up the hunt?"

Lami shook his head. "We've still got loaded rifles. They'll get us a few 'gators. Let's make tracks for the pool!"

The poachers shouldered their weapons and went through the mangroves in single file with Tom Lami in the lead.

"I'll follow them," Joe whispered to his brother. "You stay here and see if you can find out where the rangers are."

"Okay. They probably know where the alligator pool is. Let's hope they'll bring enough men to break up the hunt!"

Joe moved into the mangrove thicket where the poachers had gone, while Frank returned to their skiff. Unhooking the microphone, he called park ranger headquarters.

"Any word on the patrol boats?" he asked eagerly.

"They're close to your area," the sergeant said. "Just reported in."

"Do they know where the alligator pool is?"

"Sure. Not far from the big bend of Moss Tributary. Every ranger knows that."

"That's where the poachers are," Frank said. "We overheard them when they were talking about it."

"Good. I'll put a call through to the patrol right now and tell them." The sergeant hung up, and Frank wondered what to do while he was waiting. He decided to make sure the poachers could not escape if they got away from the rangers. He went back to the camp, picked up a tin cup from among the cooking utensils, scooped water from the stream, and poured it into the gas tank of the poachers' boat.

"That'll ground them," he told himself.

Then he stared downstream for a glimpse of the

patrol. His eyes strayed to the alligator den that had sheltered him and Joe during the storm. A huge lizard glared at him from the hiding spot!

Frank shuddered. I'm glad we didn't have *him* for a roommate last night, he thought. Just then the sound of a motor came from downstream. A small blue outboard with two men inside chugged toward the boy.

They did not look like park rangers, so Frank cautiously ducked into the undergrowth. The blue outboard pulled to a stop behind the poachers' boat. Frank recognized the man at the controls.

Mark Morphy!

"Butch, that boat belongs to Tom Lami," Morphy called out to his companion. "He and the others must be nearby. Let's wait for them here."

He stepped ashore followed by a young man with a brown beard. Both sat down under a mangrove tree.

Frank decided to keep an eye on them. I wish the rangers would get here and nab these guys, he thought.

"I'm worried about the Hardys," Morphy spoke up. "I shouldn't have left that photo of them in Raymond Wester's house. That was a stupid move. But how could I tell he'd hire them instead of having them arrested?"

"True," Butch agreed. "But why are you worried? You haven't seen them up here, have you?"

"No. But I'm sure they're not sitting in Key Blanco doing nothing!"

"They're looking for the Bolívar portrait," Butch agreed. "Where is it?"

"I don't know. Lami and Nitron helped me get it, but then I gave it to the chief."

Frank was hoping fervently that Morphy would mention the name of the elusive gang leader, but instead Wester's former secretary stood up and started pacing back and forth. "I didn't tell you this," he said. "But the Hardys broke up Nitron's smuggling racket."

"What!" Butch was flabbergasted.

"I found out just before we came here. Nitron and his men were arrested on Egret Island!"

"How did it happen?"

"The boys joined his gang pretending to be sailors and sicced the police on him."

"No wonder you're worried," Butch said. "So am I. Maybe they're after us now!"

"Well, I doubt they know about the poaching operation, but the chief is sufficiently worried to call a meeting at the stone house north of here. He wants to deal with the men on a one-to-one basis from now on to make sure no snoopers infiltrate the organization again. Also, he wants a contract out on the Hardys, so they can't butt in anymore."

"Good. I can't wait to get rid of them."

"Neither can I."

The two men fell silent. At last Morphy looked at his wristwatch. "There's no telling when Tom and his group'll be back. "I can't wait any longer. Got to meet the chief."

"I'll stay here," Butch offered.

"Good idea. Soon as they show, tell 'em to come to the stone house. The chief will give 'em their orders."

Frank's mind was racing. He wanted to follow Morphy to the gang's headquarters, but what about Joe? He decided to leave a message for his brother. He hurried back to their skiff, took his notebook out of a locker, and quickly scribbled, "Joe, follow trail north to endsville. Chief there."

He placed the note on the bow, laid a paddle over it to keep it from blowing away, and hurried back to where the two men had been talking.

Meanwhile, Butch had retreated into the blue outboard. Morphy was already passing by the dead embers of the fire, and moving in a northerly direction.

Frank circled cautiously around the camp to prevent Butch from seeing him. He made sure to leave a trail of broken branches for Joe to recognize, then he shadowed Morphy into the mangroves.

16

Giant Jaws!

Joe, in the meantime, had followed the poachers after they left their camp. The trail through the mangroves was soaked from the night's torrential downpour, and the soil mixed with dead leaves was slippery. Joe struggled to keep his balance and felt glad he was wearing heavy boots.

After an hour's trek, the group heard a roaring noise up ahead. Lami ordered his men to halt.

"Check your guns!" he commanded.

The sound of hands slapping on metal gun barrels made Joe realize the poachers were getting ready for action. Then Lami gave the order to move out. Joe stayed close behind the men.

The roar grew louder as they descended a small

hill and stopped at the last row of mangroves. While the poachers were concentrating on the view from the trees, Joe felt safe sneaking up close enough to see what they were looking at.

The land sloped down on all sides to a pool about one hundred yards across. Dozens of alligators were sunning themselves on the banks. Others were cruising through the water or snapping at fish. The alligators bellowed ferociously, and Joe realized this was the roaring sound he had heard down the trail.

Lami addressed the gang. "Each of you concentrate on one 'gator. Take careful aim so we don't waste any bullets!"

The poachers raised their rifles and got ready to fire. Thinking quickly, Joe picked up a large stone and lofted it high over the trees. It fell into the pool with a loud splash.

Instantly the alligators on the banks slithered into the pool, swam to the spot where the splash had occurred, and submerged with those already in the water.

Lami was thunderstruck. "What was that?" he demanded, lowering his rifle.

"Musta been a mangrove fruit falling in," Fatso said. "Anyway, they think it's something to eat. We'll have to wait for 'em to come up again."

Just then a swishing noise in the undergrowth

behind him caused Joe to whirl around. A giant alligator was charging at him! Its jaws were wide open revealing rows of long, jagged fangs!

Instinctively Joe grabbed a mangrove branch over his head and swung himself into the air. The lizard pounded underneath, its snapping jaws barely missing the boy's feet.

Its momentum caused it to hurtle into the gang of poachers. Screaming in terror, the men ran for safety, dropping their rifles as they fled into the underbrush. Apparently the alligator was equally scared. It careened into the pool and dove under with the rest of the lizards.

Since the poachers were scattered quite a distance away, Joe saw his chance to ruin their hunt. He dropped to the ground and raced to the spot where the rifles lay. One by one he picked them up and tossed them into the pool.

Then he darted back into the mangroves, hoping to reach safety before the poachers realized what he had done.

But it was already too late! He heard Lami yell, "That's Joe Hardy! Grab him!"

Fatso, who was closer than Joe had thought, jumped from behind a bush and collared the young detective. Breaking loose, Joe knocked him down with a karate chop. Then he got past another gang member by kicking his feet out from under him.

But a third man seized Joe in a bear hug and wrestled him to the ground.

They rolled over and over. Two other poachers rushed up and pulled Joe to his feet, holding him with his arms behind his back.

He was the gang's prisoner!

"The great Joe Hardy!" Lami snickered. "Where's your brother?"

"He'll be here any minute," Joe replied.

Fatso grinned evilly. "Good. We'll grab him, too!"

"I doubt it," Joe said. "Frank's bringing the rangers with him!"

The poachers gasped. "The rangers!" Lami snarled. "We gotta get outa here, quick!"

"Not until we take care of this snooper!" Fatso declared. "We've been saying all along we'd like to toss the Hardys to the alligators. Now let's do it!"

Lami nodded. "Good idea. He can use one of our rifles to fight off the little pets!"

The poachers guffawed at this joke, then they hustled Joe down to the shore of the pool. No movement broke its calm surface, and there was no sign of the giant lizards.

Joe shuddered. He could imagine dozens of the ferocious animals lying at the bottom, then swarming to the kill as soon as he hit the water! He had never been in a tighter spot!

"Okay," Lami said. "Let's give him the old heave-ho!"

Four of the men grabbed Joe's arms and legs and lifted him off the ground. They swung him back and forth a few times to gain momentum and were just about to let him fly through the air into the water, when three alligators surfaced right in front of them! The lizards slithered up the bank and rushed toward the gang!

In a spasm of fear, the four dropped Joe on the ground and the whole gang ran off with the alligators in hot pursuit!

One 'gator clamped its jaws on Lami's ankle, and only his thick leather boot saved him from serious injury. He kicked frantically until the lizard let go, then rushed into the mangroves.

A second 'gator attacked Fatso and caught his coat between its fangs. The coat ripped off, and the lizard swallowed it. Fatso dashed after Lami, while the third 'gator dispersed the rest of the gang by snapping its jaws and lashing its tail.

The lizards had ignored Joe in their initial pursuit of the poachers. But as he picked himself up, he saw the three alligators staring at him. A chill ran down his spine and his knees almost gave way as he realized he was trapped between the ferocious beasts and the pool!

17

Trapped!

Glaring savagely, the three alligators advanced toward Joe. There was no chance to escape!

Then, a rustling in the undergrowth caused the lizards to turn. A terrified rabbit rushed past, chased by a bobcat. When it saw the alligators, the rabbit turned and fled along the side of the pool.

Slithering forward, the alligators intercepted the bobcat, which doubled back along the route it had come. Forgetting all about Joe, the lizards chased the bobcat into the woods.

Joe ran into the mangrove forest. Having no choice, he had to take the same direction as the gang. He hoped that the men were far enough away, allowing him to find a safe hiding place.

However, two of the poachers noticed him and began to shout.

"Head him off!" Lami yelled back. "Do him in this time!"

Joe raced on, realizing some of the outlaws were behind him, and the rest ahead. He could hear them closing in on him. Gasping for breath, he looked around desperately for a spot to hide.

A mound of branches, twigs, leaves, and grass caught his eye. "An alligator's nest!" he thought. Quickly he made sure the baby alligators were gone, then climbed into the nest and pulled some of the vegetation over his head. He had to huddle up with his chin on his knees, hardly daring to breathe!

The gang came together moments later right next to him. "Where is he?" Tom exploded.

"He musta got through somehow," Fatso said. "One of the guys goofed, and he sneaked past."

The men blamed each other for Joe's escape, and argued loudly until Lami motioned for them to be quiet. "Look, he ain't here anymore," he said. "We might as well go back to camp."

"Frank Hardy and the rangers might be there," Fatso pointed out.

Lami shook his head. "I think the kid was bluffing. Anyhow, if the rangers found our camp, they'd

be headed for the alligator pool
trail so we don't run into them
return to our boat, unless one
idea of how to get out of this v

No one had, and Lami ca
very quiet and on the lookout
rangers. As they turned to leave, Tom
fell right next to the alligator nest. Joe held
breath. *Any closer, and he'll be in here with me!* the boy thought nervously.

Lami picked himself up. "That 'gator tore my boot when it grabbed my ankle," he complained. "Makes it hard for me to walk, especially on this ooze. Let's get out of here, fast!"

Joe sighed with relief when the poachers had left. He pushed aside a patch of branches and peeked out. The coast was clear, so he stood up and quickly circled around the men, trying to head them off. He wanted to get to the camp before they did, to warn Frank.

However, he ran into dense vegetation that slowed him up. In some places he had to break through tangles of vines and creepers. As a result, the gang reached their destination before him. They had stopped to discuss their next move when he arrived.

Joe surveyed the area from his hiding place

e mangroves. There was no sign of Frank
rangers.

mi had ordered two of his men to scout
ound the camp. They now came back and reported seeing no one. "But there's a blue outboard right behind our boat," one of them said.

"Must be the Hardys'," Fatso guessed. "Search it and see if there's anything that tells us what they're up to."

The men inspected the boat thoroughly. "Nothing here!" one called out.

"They covered their tracks well," Fatso declared. "But they have to come back to the boat. Let's set a trap for 'em!"

"We don't have time," Lami objected. "The rangers might be on our trail, and we have to get back to Everglades Junction to get more ammunition and guns."

"You want to resume the hunt?" one of the men asked.

"In a few days, when the heat's off," Lami said.

"Why don't we sink the Hardys' outboard?" Fatso asked.

"Good idea," Tom agreed. He was already in their own boat trying to start the engine. It came to life, coughed a few times, and died. While two of the men headed for the blue outboard, Lami made several more attempts to turn the engine over, with the same negative result.

"What's wrong with this thing?" he shouted furiously.

Fatso tore a branch from an overhanging mangrove, stripped the leaves off, and pushed it into the tank. Then he examined the discoloration where it had extended into the gasoline.

"Somebody put water in here!" he exploded. "I bet it was that Hardy kid! He did it before he sneaked up on us at the alligator pool!"

"It's always the Hardys," Lami said through clenched teeth. "We'll fix 'em!"

The poachers got out of the boat and Lami called the two men who had begun to work on the blue outboard. Excitedly, they debated what to do.

Tom had an idea. "Let's siphon off what's in the outboard and use the gas for our boat. Might be enough to get us to Everglades Junction."

Fatso grinned. "Good idea. I'm glad you guys didn't sink it yet!" Then he held up a hand, motioning for silence. "Sh! Somebody's coming!"

A hush fell over the gang. They heard footsteps approach in the distance.

"Maybe it's one of the Hardys!" Lami hissed. "Fan out—we'll trap him!"

Quickly the men moved into the woods and took

up positions behind the trees. The footsteps became louder, and a figure appeared behind the foliage. Tom and one of his cohorts leaped on him in a flash.

A second later, Lami cried out in surprise. "It's Butch! Let go of him. He works with Morphy!"

The newcomer straightened his collar where the two had gripped him. "I'm glad you noticed before slugging me," he grumbled. "I just been out looking for mangrove fruit. Got hungry waiting for you guys."

"How'd you get here?"

"Came with Morphy in the blue outboard. He went to meet the chief while I waited to fill you in."

"What's up?" Lami asked.

"We're all to go to the stone house. The chief wants to talk to us."

Lami looked surprised. "That's a switch. He always left messages and wouldn't even see me and Nitron."

"He will now," Butch said. "Nitron's been busted by a couple of spies."

"What!"

"The Hardys infiltrated his gang," Butch said, and reported what had happened.

"Those pests!" Tom exploded, then told Butch

about their encounter with Joe at the alligator pool.

"I wish we could leave right now," he concluded. "We're not safe with these kids on the loose."

"We'd better go see the chief," Butch advised. "I know the way. Follow me and be very quiet. He'll tell us what to do."

He led the gang into the woods. Joe wondered where his brother was. "He wouldn't have left without planting a clue for me," the boy thought. "But where?"

Then he had an idea. He hurried to the skiff the Hardys had hidden before sneaking up to spy on the poachers. He saw the note Frank had anchored on the bow and nodded with a grin. Next he called park ranger headquarters.

"Any word on the patrol?" he asked the sergeant.

"They were held up on the way," was the reply. "I'm not sure just when they'll be there."

"Do they know a place called the stone house?"

"I doubt it. Must be off the routes we keep under surveillance."

"There'll be a trail of broken branches going north from the poachers' camp," Joe said. "They should have no trouble finding the camp. It's just before the big bend."

"I'll alert the patrol at once," the sergeant promised, then hung up.

Joe pocketed Frank's note and went to the north side of the camp. Finding the spot where Frank had begun to shadow Morphy, he plunged into the woods. Would he find the gang's headquarters at the end of the trail?

18

Deadly Moat

Far ahead of Joe, Frank had carefully broken branches on obvious trees to show where he had gone. Each time he had chosen the lowest branch and snapped it at a point about one foot away from the tree trunk.

The Hardys often used signals to communicate with each other when they were on dangerous cases. Frank knew his brother would notice the trail and make his way in the right direction.

Keeping Morphy in sight, he found the terrain changing. The swamp of water, mud, and tropical vegetation gave way to a dry area where the footing was better. Now the earth was solid and there were as many pine trees as mangroves.

Finally, an isolated building became visible. It was three stories high, faced with Florida limestone, weather-beaten, and covered with moss. Most of the windows were shattered, and broken shutters dangled at crazy angles. The paint on the front door was peeling, and the grounds were thick with weeds.

Looks like nobody's lived here since the year one, Frank thought. He speculated that the house might have been built in the days when the United States Government considered draining large areas of the Everglades in order to open swamp area for housing. Eventually, the Everglades National Park was created instead.

"The builder jumped the gun," Frank told himself. "He erected the place, then found it was too far out in the boondocks to live in. He sure made it easy for the chief, though. What a meeting place for crooks!"

The weeds were trampled in a path to the house. Someone had been there recently.

Frank ducked into the tall weeds and followed Morphy cautiously in a panther crawl. Soon he came to a moat ten feet deep surrounding the house.

He looked over the edge and gasped. The shallow water in the moat was teeming with alligators!

He turned to see what Morphy would do. The former secretary rummaged in the underbrush and found a two-by-six. He threw it across the moat to permit a safe crossing above the alligators.

On the other side, a drop gate kept the giant lizards penned in the moat. If it were raised, it would allow them to swarm onto the grounds around the house.

Morphy placed one foot on the board to test its stability. Satisfied that it would hold him, he began to walk over it. Halfway across, he stumbled. Teetering to one side, he hovered precariously over the moat. Below him, the alligators bared their teeth and waited for him to fall!

At the last moment, however, Morphy regained his footing. He extended his arms on either side to keep his balance and walked the rest of the way across. Then he mounted the front steps and pushed in the door, which opened on creaking, rusty hinges.

He went inside and closed the door behind him. The alligators settled down again, since their prey had escaped them, but kept their eyes fastened on the board to see who would come next.

Frank considered going after Morphy, but realized he could be seen from the broken window in the front door. No sound came from inside the house. Suddenly the boy heard voices behind him. The poachers appeared from the woods and took the path up to the moat.

"I'd like to shoot these monsters," Fatso said, looking down at the alligators.

"Forget it," Tom advised him. "They're here to protect the place when the chief's away. He don't want anyone snooping around."

Lami led the way across the trench and the men followed one by one. Fatso was at the end. The thick board dipped and creaked under his weight, but he made it to the other side. The poachers went into the house, and Frank heard them being greeted by Mark Morphy. However, he was too far away to make out the ensuing conversation.

Suddenly a cry of an Everglades hawk pierced the stillness around the house. It was repeated four times at intervals of about ten seconds.

Frank grinned. He knew it was Joe—the brothers frequently located one another by simulating the sounds of animals or birds when they were out in the woods.

Frank crawled back into the trees and responded with the same cry, repeating it twice.

Minutes later Joe slipped through the mangroves and joined him. Quickly Frank explained the situation.

"Are the rangers coming?" he asked at the end.

"They're headed for the camp," Joe told him. "They don't know where the stone house is, but I told them to follow our trail. I hope they'll find it." He looked at the front of the house. "How do we get over there?" he wondered.

Frank described the moat filled with alligators. "We'll have to get across somehow," he concluded. "We can't use the board because we'd be spotted. Let's go around back and see if there's another way."

Sticking to the line of trees to avoid being seen, the Hardys circled the house. Everywhere the open moat gaped before their feet, and there was no other board to be found.

"We'll have to do some broken-field running through the 'gators," Joe quipped.

"We'd get tackled before we reached the goal line," Frank said. "Hey Joe, I have a brainstorm. Come around back again."

In the rear of the house, Frank pointed to a tall pine tree standing in the yard about halfway between the moat and the house. The stump of a branch extended upward at an angle and touched the roof.

"We could throw a rope over that branch and swing across," Frank suggested.

"Sure. Do you have one?"

"We can make one out of the vines," Frank replied.

Joe grinned. "Terrific idea."

Speedily the boys tore up thick, supple vines and tied them together. Joe tested the rope by looping it over the branch of a nearby tree and hanging on it.

"It's strong enough," he confirmed. Then he tied one end into an open knot and passed the length of the rope through the opening.

"Perfect," he pronounced. "I could lasso steers with it."

"Try to lasso the pine tree," Frank suggested.

Since there was no sign of life in the rear of the house, Joe walked boldly up to the moat. The alligators stirred at his approach and opened their jaws expectantly, but he ignored them.

Coiling the rope in one hand, he cast the lasso at the sheared-off branch of the pine tree. It fell over the stump and held fast!

"I'm glad you've got a good aim." Frank chuckled. "Otherwise we would've had to make another line. The 'gators would have eaten this one if it had dropped in the moat!"

Joe grinned and carried the end of the rope to another tall tree on their side of the moat. "We'll tie it up there at about the same level and work our way across hand over hand."

Both boys climbed the tree and Frank secured the line. Joe offered to go first. He grasped the rope, but soon realized that it was quite slippery. Clenching his teeth he strained the muscles in his arms and hands almost beyond endurance as he pulled himself over the deadly trap. Once Joe had reached the roof, Frank followed. The older Hardy boy actually lost the grip of his left hand as he was in the middle of the moat and the giant lizards snapped hungrily at his dangling body. However, he regained his hold and made it to the other side with nothing worse than a blister on his palm.

"Wow!" he gasped. "I hope we don't have to go back this way!"

"I know what you mean," Joe said as he led the way to a corner of the roof where a rainspout extended to the ground. "It was not the most pleasant means of transportation."

The young detectives silently slid down the drainpipe and jumped onto the grass. Stooping low and hugging the wall, they sneaked around the house to a side window where they could hear the gang talking.

Cautiously they peeked through the half-open pane into a dusty room with wallpaper hanging down in shreds. Bits and pieces of plaster lay on the floor. A carpet was rolled up along one wall, and chairs, tables, and a sofa were covered with sheets. A discolored spot on the floor showed where rain had leaked through a hole in the roof.

"What a spooky place," Joe whispered.

The poachers were sitting on the furniture without bothering to remove the sheets. Morphy perched on an ottoman facing the window.

"We want to poach alligators," he was saying.

"No problem," Fatso declared. "That's what the chief wants, isn't it?"

"But where do we stand now?" Tom Lami asked.

Morphy shrugged. "It's a whole new ball game."

Footsteps sounded on the board across the moat, then the door opened with a harsh creak as the newcomer entered.

"Here comes the chief now," Morphy said and got to his feet. Just then the man became visible to the Hardys. He was short and wore a hat pulled low over his forehead. Sunglasses further obscured his face. Yet, somehow he seemed familiar to the young detectives!

"Hi, Chief," Morphy greeted him.

"Hello, men. I'm glad you could all make it," the stranger responded.

It was his voice that gave him away. Frank and Joe realized at the same instant that the chief was none other than Harrison Wester!

19

Grizzly Jailers

Wester did not limp, and he walked without a cane.

"I'm changing my method of operation," he began. "As you probably know by now, Nitron has been arrested. This means a substantial loss to my business. In order to keep the poaching operation running smoothly, I feel I must take tighter control."

"This is why you came personally to talk to us today?" Tom Lami asked.

"That's right. Each group had too much autonomy as long as I only communicated by written messages. Nitron hired people without my knowledge. This was a crucial mistake and it landed him in jail."

"And all because of the Hardys," Lami muttered.

"Those snooping kids even followed us into the Everglades," Fatso said and explained how Joe had escaped at the alligator pool, and how they assumed he had immobilized the poachers' boat by pouring water in their gas tank.

"Do the Hardys know about the stone house?" Wester asked, worried.

"I don't see how they could," Lami said.

"They're smart, smarter than I thought. I'd have kept a tighter hold on them had I known," Wester admitted. "You never can tell where they'll turn up. Mark, you shouldn't have brought them into the case with that ridiculous photo you left for my brother in Bayport."

Morphy looked embarrassed. "Sorry about that, Chief," he mumbled.

"And I told you to keep the Hardys under surveillance!" Wester added angrily.

"I tried," Morphy protested. "But Frank saw me the night I came to talk to you in your house. After that, I didn't dare go near Smugglers Cove!"

"You have a point there," Wester mused. "Anyway, I left word at my house that I was in Key

West. I never thought the Hardys would figure out the Everglades angle."

He paused for a moment and bit his lip. "We'll have to clear out of here at once. Tom, I'll send Morphy to meet you in Blanco City next week and give you my further orders. Don't do anything until you hear from him, understand?"

"Yes, sir. I'll pass the word around to the men after I speak to Tom."

"Since the rangers are on your trail, you might run into them. Pretend to be campers. There's nothing that could possibly tell them what our real business was, since all your weapons and ammunition are gone."

Wester turned and walked to the window. Frank and Joe quickly flattened themselves against the wall on either side, hardly daring to breathe.

Morphy went up to the chief and said quietly, "No more smuggling? It was a great business."

"We'll build it up again later. Not until the heat's off."

"Does your brother suspect anything?"

"Raymond?" Wester snorted. "He has no idea I'm running this show. But he knows the Hardys suspect you of helping steal the picture, Mark."

Morphy shrugged. "I don't care what the Hardys think."

"Neither do I," Wester agreed. "Nevertheless, we'll have to get rid of them before we do anything else. Them and their two friends, Hooper and Morton. They're still at my house, according to my housekeeper."

"How are you going to handle it?"

"As soon as I get home, I'll have Morton and Hooper pushed off the cliff at Smugglers Cove. It'll look like an accident—a fatal one!" he added with an evil grin. "Then we'll set a trap for the Hardys."

Joe leaned forward to Frank and whispered, "We'll have to warn Chet and Biff!"

The movement caught Wester's eye; he had spotted the boys! "The Hardys are out there!" he shouted. "Don't let them get away again! Throw them into the moat with the alligators!"

The gang members rushed across the room, while the young detectives turned away from the window in fright.

"Let's climb back on the roof!" Joe urged, running toward the closest rainspout. He pulled himself up hand-over-hand, bracing his feet against the side of the house for support.

But Frank had another idea. Before joining his brother, he ran to the drop gate and lifted it until it clicked into place, creating an exit from the moat. Immediately an alligator slithered through the opening.

Frank took to his heels toward the drainpipe and climbed up just in time to escape the ferocious lizard. He heard its jaws bang together in baffled fury just below him!

The poachers, meanwhile, had rushed to the front door. Tom Lami opened it, then stopped short in surprise when he saw the yard swarming with alligators!

More lizards emerged through the drop gate and pushed across the unkempt grass. One was already waddling up the stairs to the porch and glared at the frightened poacher.

"Get back!" Lami yelled. But the men behind him who did not see the danger kept shoving forward, anxious to pursue Frank and Joe Hardy.

Lami placed his hands against the frame on either side of the door. Desperately he pushed back against those pressuring him from behind—terrified of being forced into the jaws of the alligator!

Finally the men realized what was happening and drew back into the house. As Lami slammed the door shut, the alligator that had been charging headlong across the porch ran into it with a loud crash. A panel splintered, and the animal pushed its claws through the gap in the wood.

Wester and his henchmen watched in horror as the alligator explored the hole in an effort to find a way in.

"We'd better go upstairs!" Tom screeched.

"Let's try the back door first," Morphy cried out. "Maybe we can get away over the moat if all the 'gators are out front. There's another board in the closet. We can use that to get across."

He ran through the house with the gang at his heels. Throwing the kitchen door open, he saw the yard swarming with more alligators.

Furiously, Morphy banged the door shut. "It won't work!" he called to the others. "They're all around the place!"

"Let's throw something to eat out back," Fatso proposed. "It'll distract their attention while we cross the moat!"

Wester shook his head. "I gave them the rest of my food supply when I was here last week. There's no way for us to distract them, unless somebody wants to volunteer!"

His words made the gang shudder.

On the roof, meanwhile, Frank and Joe watched the alligators swarm over the grounds.

"Don't fall," Frank warned his brother, "or you'll become an alligators' blue plate special."

"Very funny," Joe grumbled as they made their way to where the rope was tied to the tree branch. It was their only route of escape!

Suddenly a clattering sound came from the sky. Seconds later a helicopter arrived and circled overhead. On its side were the words: EVERGLADES PARK RANGERS.

The Hardys were ecstatic at the sight of the chopper. Frantically they waved to the pilot. Afraid he might not see them, Frank took a handkerchief out of his pocket, asked Joe for his, then used them as signal flags in nautical fashion. He spelled out the words: POACHERS HERE.

The helicopter swung low over the house and the pilot waved his hand to show that he understood. Then he flew off to bring in reinforcements.

"What do we do now?" Joe asked.

"We can wait here on the roof for the rangers to come, or we can go back on the rope," Frank said.

"I'm not crazy about the rope retreat," Joe decided, "but I think we should do it and kick the board off the moat so the 'gators won't be able to leave the grounds."

"You're right," Frank said. "Just hold tight so you don't become a snack for Wester's pets."

With great concentration and fierce effort the boys made their way to the tree on the other side. After resting a few minutes, they climbed down and walked to the moat. They removed the board, watching the scene from where they stood.

The alligator at the front door had stopped trying to force its way in. However, three others had arrived at the porch, and two more lay on the steps.

The rest of the dangerous lizards were roaming the grounds.

"There's a perfect jail for you," Joe declared with a chuckle. "The crooks won't come out of the house as long as the 'gators are guarding them!"

"I wouldn't either," Frank said. "Now all we have to do is wait for help."

"I hope that won't take too long." Joe sighed. "Somehow these critters make me nervous."

"Tell you what," Frank advised. "Let's go find some mangrove fruit. I'm starved."

"So am I," Joe agreed, suddenly realizing that they had had nothing to eat that morning.

They gathered enough mangroves for a snack, then sat with their backs against a tree, trying to keep their eyes open after their exhausting experience.

Finally, about an hour later, the rangers arrived. There were ten of them, led by a lieutenant, who introduced himself as Dennis Mishkin.

"We were given directions to the poachers' camp by headquarters," he said. "When we got there, we couldn't figure out which way you had gone because the area had been trampled over too much. So we called for a helicopter spotter."

"I'm glad you did," Frank said. "We were able to attract his attention."

Lieutenant Mishkin nodded. "He radioed your position to us. What's the situation now?"

The Hardys explained how the alligators had the poachers trapped in the stone house on the other side of the moat.

"We always come prepared for alligators," the lieutenant said, and ordered his men to take large pieces of meat out of a leather sack. They threw them into the water.

The alligators responded instantly. They rushed for the drop gate leading into the moat, waddling and slithering as they went. They snapped, hissed, and roared, jostling one another at the opening.

Getting through, they fell upon the meat with ravenous jaws. Hungrily they pulled it apart and devoured it in big chunks.

Joe replaced the board and ran across to the gate. He allowed it to fall to the ground, and the alligators were once again trapped in the moat!

20

The Hidden Portrait

Lami had watched what was happening through the window. "The rangers are here!" he yelled in a frenzy.

"And the Hardys are with them!" Fatso bellowed. "They've got the 'gators penned up in the moat again!"

The rest of the gang panicked. Frightened and confused, they shouted at each other. The noise rose to a crescendo as the rangers rushed the door, burst into the house, and subdued the gang.

Wester sneaked out of the room during the commotion and headed for the back door. Frank and Joe saw him, however, and ran after him into the kitchen.

The chief managed to yank the door open. He scrambled down the steps, fleeing across the yard with Joe in hot pursuit. Frank headed in the opposite direction to remove the board before Wester got there. He managed to do it just before the smuggler arrived with Joe on his heels.

Wester came to an abrupt halt on the edge of the moat. An alligator glared at him. Clawing with its hind legs on the bottom of the trench, it pushed partway up the side and opened its jaws. Three others surfaced right alongside.

"Want to swim across, Chief?" Frank asked grimly.

"You win," Wester mumbled. He turned and walked back to the house with Frank and Joe on either side making sure he did not try to escape again. The boys took him to the front room where the rangers had been searching the poachers.

"So far we haven't found anything incriminating," Lieutenant Mishkin admitted.

"Don't talk!" Wester snarled at his gang.

The rangers searched him next, and examined the notebook in his pocket. In it he had written memos to himself, but there was not a single entry that linked him to either smuggling or poaching.

"You've got nothing on me!" Wester snapped. "It's just the Hardys' word against mine. Otherwise you can't prove a thing!"

The rangers ignored him. While Lieutenant Mishkin stayed to guard the handcuffed prisoners, the other officers searched the house. However, they came up empty again, and soon returned to the living room, greatly discouraged.

Just then Frank noticed a piece of paper on the floor under a strip of loose wallpaper. He picked it up and looked at it.

The words read:

Diamond necklace—Egret Island.

"That's Wester's message to Ignaz Nitron telling him to steal Professor Viga's heirloom!" he cried out excitedly.

Joe described the alchemist's experience with the smugglers while Frank laid the paper on the table beside Wester's open notebook to compare the handwriting.

"It's the same!" he declared after studying the two samples carefully.

Lieutenant Mishkin examined the evidence. "You're right," he agreed. "This is the proof we need. But why did Wester leave a message about Egret Island out here in the Everglades?"

"Do you want to tell them about it, Chief?" Frank asked the gang leader.

"There's nothing to tell!" Wester snarled.

Mark Morphy, however, wanted to ingratiate

himself with the authorities. "If I report everything I know, will you use me as a witness and go easy on me?"

"I can't promise," the lieutenant said, "but cooperation has never hurt. Before you begin, though, let me read you your constitutional rights."

Wester glared at his accomplice, who was informed that he did not have to say anything without the advice of a lawyer. But Morphy was frightened and ready to talk.

"Mr. Wester wanted more paintings than he could afford," he said. "So he decided to go into smuggling and poaching to raise the dough."

"Shut up!" Wester grated.

Morphy paid no attention to him. "That's when he brought me into the deal," the former secretary went on. "He organized the gangs led by Nitron and Tom Lami, but he didn't want to be known to them. That's why he left their orders here in the stone house."

"How'd he ever find this place?" Frank asked.

"I don't know. It's been abandoned for decades. He just ran into it when he was out exploring the Everglades, I believe."

"And that bad limp he put on when we met him was just a fake," Joe stated.

"Sure. That way no one suspected him of getting around in the wilderness by himself."

"What happened after Nitron and Lami received their messages?" Frank asked.

"Ignaz and Tom were supposed to burn them," Morphy replied. "Only, Ignaz left this one lying around by mistake."

Wester could not contain himself any longer. "Nitron is a fool!" he exploded. "First he left a fingerprint on the wall when he took the Bolívar painting in Bayport. Then he failed to burn the Egret Island message."

"Why did you have the picture stolen when your brother was giving it to you anyway?" Frank pressed him.

"My guess is you were hoping to collect the insurance money," Joe added. "Then you'd have the money *and* the picture."

Wester's guilty look showed the Hardys Joe was right, even though he did not admit the fact.

"How did Tom Lami get your gun?" Frank asked.

"Mr. Wester gave it to me," Morphy volunteered. "I passed it on to Tom."

"Was Mrs. Summers involved in your scheme?" Joe wanted to know, remembering how suspiciously the surly housekeeper had acted.

"You kiddin'?" Morphy replied. "She doesn't even like me. Besides, she feels she's Raymond's watchdog whose mission in life is guarding his treasures. So she barks at anyone who dares enter the house."

"I have one more question," Frank said. "Where is the Bolívar portrait?"

Morphy shrugged. "I have no idea."

"And I'm not telling you!" Wester screamed. "No one knows where it is but me. If you're so smart, figure it out yourself!"

Further discussion brought no results, and Lieutenant Mishkin stood up. "We'll take these people in," he said. "Their poaching days are over." Then he turned to the Hardys.

"One of the ecological groups should give you a medal. You've helped save an endangered species, the Everglades alligator. Our chopper is back at the camp. You can have a ride to Flamingo if you want. We'll return your boat and gear later."

The Hardys decided to accept the offer. All of those in the house went outside and walked on the board across the moat where the snapping lizards lay poised below waiting for someone to fall in. But everyone made it safely to the other side.

"I'll have these 'gators transferred to the alligator pool," the lieutenant said. "That's probably where they came from, anyway."

"That's right," Morphy confirmed. "Tom and his men dug the trench on Mr. Wester's orders and then brought them here."

"We thought nobody would be able to get across," Fatso explained. "But the Hardys found a way. How'd you do it?" he asked Frank and Joe in a surly tone.

"We used a rope provided by Mother Nature, and tied it between two trees," Joe replied with a grin. "See it there?" He pointed.

Fatso squinted. "You must have seen too many Tarzan movies!"

The group trekked back to the poachers' camp. There the Hardys put their gear, including their boots, into the skiff they had rented. The poachers' craft and the blue outboard Morphy had used were still there. The rangers took them in tow and, after loading the prisoners onto the patrol launches and informing headquarters about the capture, they started down Moss Tributary.

Frank and Joe, meanwhile, boarded the helicopter.

"I'm glad I noticed you on the roof," the pilot declared.

"So are we," Frank stated emphatically. "We couldn't have handled the gang and the alligators at the same time."

The chopper took off and the boys saw how the terrain extended for mile after mile in a maze of swamps, tall grass, mangroves, and small streams meandering through the wilderness.

When they landed in Flamingo, the boys shook hands with the pilot. "Thanks for the ride," Frank said. "We really appreciate not having to come back the slow way with our boat."

The pilot grinned. "It was a pleasure. Next time you're in the Everglades, don't forget to look us up. And if we're ever troubled by poachers again, we'll call you!"

After eating a hearty meal of roast beef sandwiches and cole slaw, the Hardys caught the ferry to Key Blanco.

"How about that creep Wester stealing the picture from his own brother!" Joe commented.

Frank nodded. "It'll be an unbelievable shock to Raymond when he finds out. And to top it all off, we haven't been able to come up with the portrait!"

Once the ferry docked in Blanco City, the boys walked to the Wester home on Smugglers Cove. The housekeeper opened the door.

"We heard about Mr. Wester's arrest on the radio!" she sputtered. "Oh, this is just terrible. We had no idea about his criminal activities, believe me!"

"Harrison Wester was very smart," Frank said. "He covered his tracks extremely well."

"Until you boys uncovered them," the housekeeper said.

"We happened to find his headquarters in the Everglades," Frank replied modestly. "But the credit for his arrest goes entirely to the park rangers. By the way, are Chet and Biff here?"

"Yes. They're out on the patio."

The boys found their friends reclining in wicker chairs watching the sunset. Chet jumped up when he saw them. "Welcome back!" he boomed. "We hear you cracked the case!"

The Hardys told their friends what had happened and Chet beamed.

"I'm proud of you!" he exclaimed. "Too bad we didn't have a chance to help. It was no fun to be stuck in this place with nothing to do, you know."

"You don't look unhappy to me." Joe pointed to a tall glass of lemonade and a plate showing the remnants of cherry pie. "Matter of fact, I think you enjoyed your vacation."

"I admit we did a little skin diving," Chet said sheepishly. "Figured we'd check out the terrain before you got back. You'll join us, won't you?"

"Sounds great," Joe said. "But our case isn't finished."

Biff banged his fist in the palm of his other hand. "You haven't found the picture!"

"That's right," Frank replied. "Wester admits that he arranged the theft, but he didn't tell us what he did with the portrait."

"Well, at least you cleared *yourselves,*" Chet spoke up. "Even if you don't know where the painting is, you can prove you didn't take it!"

"We haven't given up on it yet," Joe declared.

"But you don't know where to look," Chet said. "Seems to me you're fresh out of clues."

The Hardys nodded glumly. Not only were they disappointed about their failure, they were also wondering if another case would ever come their way. They had no idea that soon they would travel to the South Pole to solve the mystery of *The Stone Idol.*

Suddenly Joe jumped up. "Wait a minute, fellows," he said. "I just had a brainstorm. Come with me!" He led the way to the living room fireplace. Reaching up, he unhooked the landscape from the wall and examined it.

"What on earth are you doing?" Biff asked.

"Checking the frame," Joe replied. "As I suspected, it's been taken apart." He applied pressure at the joints and tried to separate it at the corners. The landscape stayed in place, but another canvas fell to the floor from behind!

Joe retrieved it and held it up. His companions saw the face of a man with sharp features, black hair, and a stern expression. He wore an old-fashioned military uniform with a high collar and epaulets on the shoulders.

"I don't believe it!" Chet cried out. "Is this the Bolívar portrait?"

"It sure is," Frank said. "I've seen pictures of him in books. That's what he looks like."

Biff scratched his head. "How did you know where to find it, Joe?"

"Wester's an art collector," the boy replied. "I was sure he wanted to keep the picture and hide it in a safe place after collecting the insurance money."

"But he has a lot of paintings," Chet spoke up. "What made you check this particular one?"

"Remember the first night we were here? He mentioned then that the missing painting was the same size as the landscape, and that he wanted to hang them side by side. Then he said, 'I can just see it now.' That was a private joke on us!"

"Of course!" Chet slapped his forehead with the palm of his right hand. "Why didn't I think of that?"

Frank grinned, then surveyed the portrait. "Simón Bolívar," he said. "The Liberator of South America!"

"Liberated by Joe Hardy!" Biff added.